"The soone
the better.

Thea's voice revealed her anxiety.

"Back where it's safe—where you're not likely to be tempted, Thea?" Dave's tone was light enough, but had an underlying edge. "Are you likely to scream if I come to your room later on? Or must I remember to bring along a gag?"

"Dave, stop it," Thea replied on an unsteady note. "You're not being funny."

"I never intended to be." His glance was fleeting, but long enough to reveal purpose in his gray eyes. "It's more than time you learned what it's all about."

"More comparisons?" she got out, refusing to take the threat seriously. "The professional versus the amateur? I can tell you now which I'd prefer."

"You can tell me anything you like," he retorted. "Proving it is something else."

KAY THORPE

the new owner

Harlequin Books

TORONTO • LONDON • LOS ANGELES • AMSTERDAM
SYDNEY • HAMBURG • PARIS • STOCKHOLM • ATHENS • TOKYO

Harlequin Presents first edition September 1982
ISBN 0-373-10534-7

Original hardcover edition published in 1982
by Mills & Boon Limited

CHAPTER ONE

It was gone seven when Thea rounded the end of the quay, and the *Molly* was already preparing to cast off, her engines raising their customary racket. The deck-hand about to let go the for'ard mooring waved an acknowledging hand in answer to her shout and desisted in his efforts, greeting her hasty approach with a grin.

'Nearly didn't make it this time,' he observed in strong West Country accents as she made for the gangway now being lowered again. 'Cutting it mighty fine!'

'My watch stopped,' she called back. 'I must have forgotten to wind it.'

'Anybody not aboard in half a minute gets left,' roared a voice from the bridge housing. 'That means you, girl!'

Thea skipped nimbly up the boarded walkway, wing-ing a smile at the grizzled head visible in the wheelhouse. 'Thanks for waiting!'

'You're lucky,' came the dour retort, and the head disappeared, leaving her to sink to a seat on the port side of the deck, the smile still lingering about her lips.

It was only then that she became aware of the man seated opposite, arms spread comfortably along the rail behind him. He was very dark, with hard-boned, deeply tanned features, his mouth at present faintly curved as if in response to her own amusement. She knew at once who he must be, and felt her smile fade abruptly, draw-ing a slight lift of one eyebrow. After almost three months of waiting the reality was both more and less than she had anticipated. The details Gavin had given her had included the fact that David Barrington was only a matter of six years or so older than his own twenty-eight years, yet she had still imagined an older man, red and burly as farmers were so often apt to be. The new owner of Sculla was far from the farmer type in any respect, his body lean yet muscular in the well-cut slacks and matching shirt, his hands long-fingered, with a tensile strength where they gripped the rail.

'Do I need to introduce myself?' he asked unexpectedly, revealing the tell-tale South African accent. 'Or do I take it my fame went before me?'

Thea returned the grey gaze with an equanimity she was far from feeling, aware that her scrutiny had been over-long, and over-critical. 'I know who you are, Mr Barrington,' she said formally. 'Everyone will know who you are. We don't get too many strangers on Sculla.'

'With no airstrip and a two-hour boat journey I'm not surprised,' he came back. 'A small plane would be an asset.'

'Or a helicopter,' she agreed smoothly. 'Then you wouldn't even need the landing strip. The estate can certainly afford it.' She bit her lip, instantly regretting the retort. 'I'm sorry,' she added on impulse. 'That was unforgivable.'

'If it was unforgivable there isn't much point in apologising,' he pointed out, sounding unmoved. 'From what I'm given to understand, it's no more than the truth. Whichever of my ancestors set up the Barrington trust seems to have known what he was about. Even the government taxes failed to break the bank.'

He was telling her nothing she didn't already know, but he couldn't be expected to realise that. That there was purpose behind his frankness was revealed when he added succinctly, 'That should put a stop to any speculation regarding the immediate future. Sculla will keep her independence.'

'You intend staying on to run the estate?' Thea asked.

'I haven't decided yet. I've a place of my own in Natal. Maybe that should come first.'

'Perhaps it should.' Thea tried to keep any eagerness from her voice, but knew she had failed to do so when she saw his eyes narrow a fraction. In an effort to retrieve the situation, she added swiftly, 'It's said one's home is where the heart is, and yours can hardly be here in England. You weren't even born in the country.'

'Seems my family history is pretty common knowledge,' he returned with an edge of irony. 'Hardly surprising, I suppose, on an island the size of Sculla. There can't be much else to do but gossip.'

Thea set her lips against the sharp retort, conscious of a certain element of truth in what he said. She had never personally found life on Sculla boring, but there were others of her age group who had and did, especially after once glimpsing the kind of life led by their contemporaries on the mainland. Compared with the attractions to be found in Penzance alone, Sculla's two pubs and weekly social hardly came up to scratch.

Yet there were so many other compensations if one only cared to look for them. On Sculla the seasons themselves brought change enough for anyone with imagination and a love of beauty. Village life suited Thea, with its slow pace and occasional minor dramas. Her parents' insistence that she attend school on the mainland from the age of eleven had caused her much heartache, although she had learned to appreciate the advantages of a more comprehensive education than the island school could provide. She had even seen the sense in staying on to take a course in business studies, but only because of Douglas Barrington's promise to find her a job on the estate as soon as she qualified: a promise he had kept by instructing his manager Tim Riley to take her on as a replacement for the secretary he had lost through marriage and subsequent motherhood. That had been almost five years ago, and the master of Sculla was dead now, the estate bequeathed by line of descent to this man seated opposite her instead of the one who surely merited it most. Gavin might only be Douglas Barrington's stepson, but Sculla was his home, and had been for almost twenty years. The newcomer was not only a total stranger, he was also a usurper.

The Barrington brothers had been in their late twenties when the split had occurred, Gregory, the younger of the two, taking himself off to South Africa to found his own branch of the family. Left childless by the death of his first wife, Douglas had lost little time in marrying again, this time to a widow with living proof of her ability to bear children in the shape of an eight-year-old son. Fate, however, had not seen fit to bless the union, and after a time Gavin had become the son Douglas longed for. Schooling had interrupted that relationship too, but at twenty Gavin had returned to Sculla for good, working alongside Tim Riley to learn the management of the estate and island finances and eventually taking over when the older man retired.

Douglas's death from a heart attack at the age of seventy-five had come as a shock to all regardless. He had seemed indestructible—a man who had discovered the secret of, if not eternal youth, certainly late middle-age. Janine Barrington had been distraught at the loss, and by all accounts even more so at the discovery that the island and trust passed by automatic decree to the only son of the long-deceased brother. Now David Barrington was here, and the only hope left was that he might not see fit to stay. True, Sculla could never belong wholly to Gavin, but he would at least retain control.

Thinking about Gavin brought a pleasant warmth to Thea's heart. He was such a fine man. She was lucky to have him feel the way he did about her. Love had blossomed slowly between them, stemming from a mutual respect and a long acquaintance. The first time he had kissed her she had been both surprised and uncertain, but it hadn't taken long to break down any barriers between them. They were planning to get engaged this coming Christmas, with his mother's blessing already bestowed, if somewhat reluctantly, on the union.

Sitting there, she was unaware of the way in which the fast lowering sun haloed her reddish-gold curls. There was speculation in the eyes of the man opposite as they rested on the small fine features, a certain deliberation in the way he moved his gaze downwards over her slender figure, lingering on the firm, unfettered points of her breasts under the cotton shirt. Coming back to earth, Thea met the grey regard and felt her customary composure momentarily desert her. So that was what it felt like to be undressed at a glance! She had never really believed it could happen before. Gathering her resources, she returned the look equably, seeing the strong mouth curve a little at the corners.

'Point taken,' he said. 'I gather you live on Sculla full time?'

'All my life,' she admitted coolly.

'Don't you find it lonely?'

'No,' she said. 'Why should I?'

'I'm asking you.'

Her shrug was deliberate. 'It depends on the mentality. Some people would be lonely in the middle of a city.'

'Sometimes cities can be the loneliest places on earth,' he countered. 'There can't be a great deal of entertainment for people of your age on an island ten by three.'

'I'm twenty-three,' she retorted with dignity. 'I don't have need for any kindergarten activities.'

'So what do you do in the evenings?'

'Walk,' she said. 'And talk. We have a discussion group once a week, and on Saturdays there's the social at the school hall.'

'So much excitement.' The mockery was light. 'The birthrate must be pretty high.'

Thea ignored that sally as beneath contempt. The new owner of Sculla wasn't going to last long, that was for certain. His kind craved the bright lights. The fact that he was already a farmer himself and therefore hardly likely to have too much time for loose living she chose to gloss over. There was farming and farming. Perhaps his kind left most of the work to a manager. Certainly someone had to be looking after the place for him right now.

'Tell me about Sculla,' he said suddenly. 'I got few details from the lawyers bar the financial aspect. I suppose they took it for granted I'd know the rest.'

'And you don't?' She was surprised and a little suspicious. 'Are you having me on?'

'Not that I'd noticed.' His tone was bland. 'Dad never spoke much about the past. Being the younger son, I imagine, he resented the way things were done.'

'It wasn't exactly a fair division,' Thea agreed. 'But there can only ever be one master of Sculla. If you had died before Douglas the inheritance would have passed to your eldest son.'

'Supposing I only had daughters?'

'I'm not sure,' she admitted. 'That could be one for the lawyers to decide. Under modern law I imagine a daughter would have equal right to inherit.'

His mouth widened briefly. 'Thanks for the run-down. I'm not married, and I don't have any offspring—not that I know of. Does that answer the question?'

Thea's glance would have frozen a lesser man to the marrow. 'Mr Barrington, I'm not in the least bit interested in your marital status,' she declared. 'Nor in your possible parental obligations either, for that matter!'

'Fine,' he returned imperturbably. 'Just so long as we have everything in the clear. You were going to tell me about Sculla.'

She took a long, steadying breath before replying, conscious of how close she had come to losing her temper—something she rarely did. 'Sculla became privately owned in the late eighteenth century,' she began in the manner of a schoolmarm imparting information to a class, 'although the Barringtons didn't come into the picture until around 1800. It's rumoured that Harry Barrington won the island in a game of cards, but it's never been proved. It's more likely that he bought the place at a give-away price because the owner at that time needed hard cash rather than land. Anyway, he was the one who had the foresight to set up the trust that keeps the estate itself independent of financial support from island produce. There are twelve farms which all pay rental, and the village is owned and maintained by Whirlow.'

'Whirlow?' The question came soft as if he were reluctant to interrupt her flow.

'The name of the house. Now your new home—at least for the present. Harry Barrington renamed it—after what I'm not sure.'

'You seem to have a special interest in the Barrington history.'

If ever there had been a moment to reveal her connection with the family this was it, yet somehow Thea couldn't bring herself to take advantage of it. Her shrug was dismissive. 'I learned most of it at the village school.

After all, we who live on Sculla owe our livelihood to the Barringtons.'

'Including your parents?'

'My father, yes. He's the island doctor.'

'That can't keep him so busy.'

'We have a population of one hundred and sixty,' she came back shortly. 'He isn't exactly run off his feet, but he has enough to keep him going. Fortunately he never wanted a practice that would bring in more than he needed to keep the household going.'

The dark head moved again, this time without mockery. 'No criticism intended. How long has your family been on Sculla?'

'Since about ten years before I was born. Dad came first. Mom is related to some people on St Mary's. They met when he was over there giving a second opinion on a case. He married her three weeks later.'

'Romantic.'

'Yes,' she said firmly, 'it was. They were both in their forties when I was born, which was a bit late, I suppose, but I wouldn't change them for a younger pair.'

'Odd,' he commented. 'My father was forty when I came into the world. I wouldn't have changed him either.'

'And your mother?' The question was out before she could stop it, born of a curiosity she could not have explained.

The faint contraction of his jawline was the only sign he gave. 'They were divorced before I was old enough to decide.'

The breeze had freshened since they had left the shelter of the little bay, cutting through the thin cotton shirt Thea was wearing. She fished a sweater out of the bag at her side and pulled it on, emerging tousle-headed to find the grey eyes on her with an odd, almost unnerving expression.

'Any chance of a drink aboard this tub?' he asked. 'It looks like being a long voyage.'

'There's usually some coffee going in the galley,' Thea told him. 'Cap'n George doesn't allow alcohol on board.' Her smile was fleeting. 'Except for medicinal purposes. Maybe if you tried passing out he could be persuaded to part with a tot of whisky.'

'Too much trouble,' he conceded. 'I'll settle for the coffee, and a sheltered spot to drink it. Is it always this cool in summer?'

'Strictly speaking, summer doesn't start for another three weeks,' Thea said, 'but it's usually cooler at sea in the evening anyway. You can go below if you like. There's a small saloon for passengers.'

'Come with me,' he invited. 'You look ready for a warm drink yourself.'

About to refuse, Thea abruptly changed her mind. There was little point in trying to evade the man, after all. 'All right.'

The saloon was, as she had said, small, but it was comfortable, with padded seats and two tables bolted to the deck for safety. Jackson Taylor, the galley hand, brought them the coffee, charging twenty-five pence a cup without batting an eyelid. Thea said nothing right then, but resolved to have a private word with the youth as soon as she had the opportunity. Nobody welcomed the new owner, it was true, but that was no excuse to start fleecing him.

The sea had roughened to a more than moderate swell, rolling the *Molly* beneath them with a movement totally lacking in any kind of synchronisation. Thea watched her companion from beneath her lashes, waiting for the all-too-familiar signs to appear. The *Molly* was notorious for eliciting green-featured malaise in even the hardiest of sailors. Only those accustomed to her peculiar gait could withstand it.

'If I have to ask where the heads are it will only be for the normal reason,' David Barrington said suddenly without lifting his eyes from the liquid he was stirring. 'I got my sea-legs in a harder school than this.'

'Bully for you.' She was not about to be put down by his easy reading of her mind. 'You live near the sea?'

'Close enough to make it pretty often. I was educated down at the Cape, and the seas there would harden off any stomach.' He looked up then. 'How about you? Do you sail?'

'A little,' she admitted. 'The currents around Sculla can be a bit tricky. Your uncle had a four-berth cruiser. She's been laid up since he died.'

'Then we'll have to resurrect her.' The pause was brief. 'Maybe you'd like to crew for me one weekend.'

Thea made a noncommittal murmur, wondering if that invitation would still stand when he discovered the truth. She should tell him, of course, but she still couldn't find the words. He would know soon enough anyway. Gavin would be at the jetty to meet her. He always was on the occasions when she returned from a trip to the mainland—and vice-versa.

'Did you want some more coffee?' she asked, watching him drain the cup. 'Jack has a potful back there.'

'We'll both have some more,' he announced in tones loud enough to reach the ears of the youth in question.

He was silent while Jackson poured the hot black liquid. Only when the latter held out a none-too-clean palm for the money did he react, lifting his head to look the other directly in the eye.

'Let's call this one on the house, shall we?'

Thea stifled a chuckle at the expression on the younger man's face, mentally chalking up a point to the newcomer, who was obviously not as easily taken in as she had thought. Jackson muttered something under his breath as he turned away, but he wasn't stopping to argue about it. Thea couldn't blame him. Standing, David Barrington was a couple of inches over six feet, with a breadth of shoulder to balance his height. A formidable opponent when roused, there was no doubt.

'Congratulations,' she said sotto voce. 'You just proved yourself a man of insight.'

'Did I?' He looked amused. 'As a matter of fact, you gave the game away drawing in your breath the way you did. For all I knew, twenty-five pence was the recognised price for a cup of coffee in these parts.'

'But you weren't going to let him get away with it once you realised.'

A gleam sprang fleetingly in the grey eyes. 'I don't let anyone get away with anything. An eye for an eye, that's my motto.'

'I see.' There was a brief silence, then Thea stirred restlessly, pushing the barely tasted coffee to one side. 'I'm going up to have a word with Cap'n George.'

David Barrington made no attempt to follow her, much to her relief. There was too much about the man that disconcerted. She needed time to regain her equilibrium.

George Yelland's greeting was as casual as might be expected of a man who had known her all her life, who had dandled her on his knee as a child and on more than one occasion chased her off his boat in the company of other would-be sailors. The *Molly* was his second craft since those days, plying the same route twice a day when the weather allowed, carrying passengers and goods from island to mainland and back again as a supplementary to the regular, inter-island boat which called at Sculla only once a week.

'Thought you'd decided to spend the night,' he added gruffly by way of apology for almost leaving her behind. 'Not like you to be late for sailing.'

'I know. I just lost track of time.' Thea was looking ahead through the screen at the sun-gilded water. 'There's quite a swell getting up. Are we in for a spell of bad weather?'

'Going to be a bit of a blow later tonight,' he conceded. 'Nothing to get worked up about. How do you find him, then?'

'Shrewd,' Thea admitted. 'And very sure of himself.'

George digested that in silence for a moment or two, big hands firm on the wheel. 'Does he plan on staying?' he asked at length.

'I honestly couldn't say what his plans might be. I don't think he's made up his mind either way yet.'

'So you and Gavin are going to have to wait and see, eh?'

'It doesn't really affect me the same way,' she said carefully. 'Gavin's the one whose future is at stake. If David Barrington does decide to stay there isn't going to be room for both of them—unless he prefers to leave the management to someone else. On the other hand, it isn't all that likely he'll want to stay. I'd say our Mr Barrington likes the kind of spare-time entertainment Sculla can't provide. Wine, women and song, that's more *his* style!'

George chuckled into his beard. 'How about beer, the church choir and a few pretty girls?'

'Hardly an adequate substitute. Sculla girls don't play the kind of games he's used to playing. He actually bragged about the number of women he's played around with.' That was unfair and she knew it, but something in her dictated the words. 'Not married, and proud of the fact!'

'Sounds like a man who might have sown a few wild oats in his time,' George agreed. 'He'll get short shrift if he tries it on with any of our lasses, own the place or not!'

Thea had the grace to feel somewhat ashamed of herself. She was giving entirely the wrong impression of the man. 'He's going on thirty-five,' she tagged on. 'Maybe he's ready to settle down now.'

'With the right girl, you mean?' The laugh was hearty. 'Pity you got yourself all tied up with young Gavin. You could have married him yourself and turned him into an islander.'

'No, thanks.' Her tone was almost brusque. 'Whoever marries David Barrington would have my deepest sympathy. He'd want to be the boss all the way through!'

'And so would any man worth his salt,' came the blunt reply. 'Trouble with you, young Thea, is you never met any man you couldn't twist round your little finger before.'

'Including you?' she queried, tongue in cheek, and received an ironic glance.

'Only so far. I'm too old to be led by the nose.'

It was a moment before she found an answer to that one. When she did speak her tone was subdued. 'You think that's what I do with Gavin?'

'Not deliberately. You're the stronger personality of the two, though, and that's not good. Takes a man to wear the trousers.'

'Gavin is a man,' she defended. 'A gentleman. He doesn't need to start beating his chest to impress me.'

'Just so long as you're happy.'

Of course she was happy, Thea told herself stoutly. Who wouldn't be with Gavin for a future husband? Old George was talking through his hat. Either that or he was simply teasing her again. His sense of humour was at best distorted.

She stayed in the wheelhouse for the rest of the trip, reluctant to face the man below again. Sculla came into view at last, long and low-lying in the foreground, with a ridge of hills forming the backbone. The sea was rougher now, running four to six foot swells before the rising wind. Admit it she would not, but Thea could feel the faint stirring of nausea and was glad that home was only a matter of minutes away.

David Barrington came up from the saloon as the *Molly* slid in alongside the stone jetty, a casual suede jacket stretched across his shoulders. He was carrying a suitcase which must have been stored out of sight below along with the jacket, for Thea certainly had noticed neither. She moved up reluctantly to his side at the rail as they waited for the gangway to be lowered, weathering his sardonic glance with an outer indifference.

'It must have been a long few words,' he commented. 'One hour and fifteen minutes, I make it.'

'I like being in the wheelhouse,' she said. 'Especially on the rougher trips. Cap'n George says there's going to be a storm later on. Good thing you arrived in time for tonight's boat. It isn't unknown for the island to be cut off for a couple of days even at this time of year.'

He made no answer, his eyes on the shore. 'I didn't think there'd be any cars on Sculla. Who does that belong to?'

'You,' she said, following his gaze to where the Marina stood waiting at the landward end of the jetty. 'Your uncle had it shipped out several years ago for his stepson to use—he was given to the occasional extravagant gesture. It should last a lifetime on the mileage it does.'

'Are the roads geared to motorised traffic?'

'Not really. But a couple don't cause too much concern. My father has one too.'

'Your father needs it. I can't really see why my stepcousin should have to ride in style.'

'It's either that or leave it to rot in the stables,' she defended swiftly. 'He has petrol brought out from the mainland at his own expense.'

The grey eyes came back to her slender figure, undergoing a change of expression in the process. 'You seem to know a lot about everything.'

It was too late for explanations because Gavin himself was even now advancing along the jetty, fair hair blowing in the wind. The gathering cloud was bringing darkness early, shutting out the reddened western skies. It was like an omen, Thea thought, stilling a sudden involuntary little shiver. The wind of change.

CHAPTER TWO

SHE went down the gangway ahead of her companion, returning Gavin's kiss with selfconscious decorum.

'The new owner's here,' she murmured for his ears only before stepping back and turning to where the other man waited. 'Mr Barrington, this is Gavin Grant.'

Almost unconsciously she found herself comparing the two men as they eyed one another. Gavin was the shorter by at least three inches, and slighter of frame, his clean-cut good looks almost boyish beside the lean cynicism of the other man's features. He gathered himself together with an obvious effort, holding out a hand with a brief, formal smile.

'Glad to see you at last. We never got any message you were on your way.'

'Possibly because I never sent one,' came the unapologetic reply. 'Does it make any difference?'

'Not at all,' Gavin hastened to assure him. 'It's just that after three months we'd almost given you up.'

'I had other affairs to take care of.' David Barrington looked back to Thea, expression difficult to define. 'Rather more than a bare detail to leave out, wasn't it?'

'I didn't think it particularly relevant,' she said, determined not to be stampeded into excuses of any kind. 'Perhaps I should have told you I'm also your estate manager's secretary.'

'Maybe I'd better know your name too.' He sounded sardonic. 'Just for the record.'

'Thea Ralston,' she said. 'You didn't ask.' For the first time she allowed the animosity to show through. 'You'd better take Mr Barrington home, Gavin. I'll walk up to the village.'

'There's room in the car for all of us,' the newcomer

pointed out. 'It can hardly be much of a detour to drop you off.'

It would have been both childish and churlish to refuse, and Thea had no wish to display either characteristic. 'Thanks,' she said.

There was barely room for three to walk abreast up the jetty, so she went ahead, aware of the two pairs of eyes resting on her back, though with obviously different sentiments. David Barrington was annoyed by her failure to communicate her position to him during their conversational exchange and wasn't bothering to conceal it, though what real difference it made to him she failed to see. She could hardly be classed a fortune-hunter under the circumstances. All Gavin had was the few thousand left him by his stepfather, who had not possessed a large personal fortune, plus a job which depended entirely on the whim of the new owner. If David Barrington decided to stay on there was relatively little doubt but that he would want full control of the estate in his own hands. Even given the opportunity, Gavin would find it difficult to accept orders from a man only six years his senior after making his own decisions for so long. Douglas had tended to leave everything to his stepson these last few years.

Still, it might not come to that, Thea comforted herself. The climate alone would probably be enough to make any radical change of life-style unpalatable to the other man. One winter here should settle the matter should there be any doubt in his mind at all. That wasn't so long to wait.

It was David Barrington who opened the rear door of the car for her, standing there holding it until she was settled in her seat, then closing it again with a brief nod to get into the front passenger seat himself, shoulders broad under the suede jacket.

'How long have you two been involved?' he asked, watching Gavin close the boot through the driving mirror.

'About twelve months,' Thea acknowledged, resenting the manner in which the question had been put. 'Do you object?'

The grey eyes shifted to meet hers through the mirror, dark brows lifting. 'Any reason why I should?'

'None at all,' she came back coolly. 'It's just the way you sounded.'

'Inflections can be deceptive.'

There was no time for more, because Gavin was sliding into the driving seat, his face set in lines which Thea, at least, recognised as determination to make the best of a bad situation. She wanted to lean forward and put her arms about him in approbation. He was handling this in exactly the right way—the only way.

The village proper lay a bare half mile inland from the little harbour, its main street running straight through between twin rows of red-tiled buildings, no two exactly alike. There was Ewles, the grocery; the post office next door; Joy's, the sole hairdresser on the island, who was always in demand. Right at the end, set back behind a garden ablaze with her mother's favourite azaleas, was her own home with its built-on surgery wing. Not an imposing residence, Thea would be the first to admit, but it was her birthplace and as such held a special place in her heart.

'See you tomorrow,' said Gavin through his opened window as she hopped nimbly out of the back before either man had chance to make a move. His smile held an element of strain. 'Usual time?'

Sunday was a day off for most people, Thea reminded herself, catching David Barrington's eye. No reason at all why Gavin should have to stick around the house just because his step-cousin had arrived home. 'Of course,' she agreed. 'I'll pack lunch, then we don't have to get back too soon.' There was a faint challenge in the tilt of her head as she looked directly at her new employer. 'Thanks for the ride. It was appreciated.'

His answering nod was perfunctory, smacking of indifference. 'Don't mention it.'

Margaret Ralston was in the small, bright kitchen putting the finishing touches to an iced cake still on its turntable in the middle of the scrubbed deal table. At sixty-two she had very little grey in the luxuriant hair a shade or two darker than her daughter's, which owed its fashionable streaked effect to over-exposure to whatever sun was going rather than Joy's attentions. There was a strong resemblance between mother and daughter, although the former lacked the stubbornness of chin inherited from John Ralston. Her greeting was as casual as if Thea had simply slipped out a few minutes before.

'Supper's ready any time you are. Chicken salad and strawberries—all right?'

'Sounds good,' Thea agreed. 'Is that for tea tomorrow?'

'I'd think so. You did say you wanted to ask Gavin, didn't you? It's his favourite kind.'

'He might not be able to make it,' said Thea. 'David Barrington has just arrived. I suppose he's going to want to go through all the books some time.'

'Time enough on Monday for that,' rejoined her mother comfortably. 'Why not invite him along too, if you think he might like company? I gather you both came over with George?'

'Yes, but I hardly think he's the type to appreciate Sunday high tea.'

'You got to know him well enough in two hours to figure that out?' Margaret's tone was mild. 'He must be a very open character.'

Thea grinned, accepting the rebuke in the same spirit. 'No, he isn't. I'm just feeling particularly rebellious about him, that's all. He holds Gavins's future in the palm of his hand, and I doubt if it's a very caring one.'

'You can't be sure until he comes right out and says what he plans on doing about Sculla. Why not give him the benefit of the doubt until then?'

She was right, and Thea knew it, yet she still couldn't bring herself to accept it like that. The sooner David Barrington realised just how the majority of the islanders felt about him the sooner he might decide to go on home. And if it was up to her he was going to find out pretty quickly. Why bother to conceal the fact?

John Ralston came in while she was eating supper, his tall, spare frame slightly stooped as it always was, as if in an attempt to minimise his height. His thin features had a worried cast, emphasising the lines about mouth and eyes yet still failing to make him look his sixty three years.

'I'm going to have to get young Paul Morrow over to the mainland,' he said. 'He isn't responding to treatment the way he should. I'd have sworn it was the same virus the other kids had, but they're all healthy as hunters again while he's still lying there like something the cat dragged in. They'll need to do some lab tests to tie it down.'

'Could it be dangerous?' asked Thea in concern. 'To Paul, I mean?'

Her father shook his head, sinking into a spare chair and accepting a mug of steaming hot cocoa from his wife with a grateful smile. 'I don't think so. Not unless he's developed a totally new strain of delayed action bug. I just don't like feeling so helpless to help, if you see what I mean. Nora doesn't like the idea of letting him go, only she can hardly leave the rest to fend for themselves while she goes with him.'

'Anything I can do?' Thea offered. 'Obviously Paul would prefer his mother with him, if anyone, but I could certainly go over with him and see him settled.'

'Nice thought,' her father rejoined, 'but I don't think Nora would take you up on it. She's the kind who has to do everything herself—you know that.' He shook his head again, this time with decisiveness. 'It will work out. It will have to. I'll take him over myself, he isn't ill enough to call out the emergency service.'

'David Barrington seems to think the island could do with a helicopter service all of its own,' said Thea with deliberation. 'Maybe he'll see fit to provide one.'

'So he arrived at last.' John sounded interested. 'What kind of man is he?'

'Difficult to tie down exactly,' Thea returned, catching her mother's glance. 'Competent, for certain. And very self-assured.'

'At his age we all were,' quipped her father humorously. 'I'll have to go over and see him. Quite a few things need looking into on Sculla, things I could never get Douglas to do anything about.'

'You should have got Gavin to speak to him,' Thea said swiftly. 'He knew how to get round him, if anyone did.'

'Not when it came to spending any real money on a long-term basis. Gavin was only a figurehead and he knew it. He's no better off now unless this new man turns over control. Think there's any chance?'

Thea shrugged. 'Your guess is as good as mine. Perhaps he'll be more forthcoming for one of his own sex.'

'From which I take it you didn't exactly hit it off with him on first sight,' chuckled her father. 'You're going to have to watch your step if you want to keep your job. Not all employers are as tolerant as Douglas was. Just remember there aren't any other secretarial posts on Sculla, and you'd hate to move to the mainland permanently.'

'I'll remember,' Thea promised. 'It all depends on what happens to Gavin, doesn't it? I can't see him wanting to stay on under someone who knows nothing at all about the place.'

'And I can't see his mother wanting to move regardless of who's in charge,' put in Margaret. 'Whirlow is her home. She has a right to go on living there—they both have.'

'Not by law,' John Ralston said mildly. 'The whole estate and island come under the trust. That means David Barrington has the last word in every sense. If he wanted them to go they would have to go. It's unfortunately as simple as that. Not that I can see any man being quite so hard-hearted.'

Thea could. When it came to the man she had met on the boat anything could happen.

George's blow blew itself out before dawn, leaving a rapidly clearing sky and a promise of a fine day to come.

Gavin arrived promptly at nine-thirty to pick her up, looking rather less unhappy than Thea anticipated.

'He isn't so bad,' he acknowledged grudgingly in answer to her question. 'He told Mother that whatever decision he eventually made, she and I would always have a home here on Sculla.'

'The least he could do,' Thea commented, determined not to revise last night's summing up too far. 'He didn't want the car today?'

'No. He said he'd take one of the horses to have an initial look round. Suppose he's more used to horseback where he comes from.'

'I didn't get the impression his farm was that far out in the wilds.' She hesitated before adding casually, 'You know, I wouldn't mind going horseback a little more often. Lady doesn't get nearly enough exercise.'

'I still don't know why you bought her,' said Gavin, ignoring the former comment. 'You had a choice of four from Whirlow.'

'Except that Lady's only just round the corner from home.' Her tone was mild. 'Anyway, she was too good a bargain to miss. Mrs Templeton was more interested in finding her a good home than the actual financial return.'

'You think they'll ever come back?' Gavin asked, momentarily sidetracked. 'He seemed so settled here.'

'I suppose he was, but there was nothing for her.' Thea shook her head decisively. 'They won't be back, not if they want to keep their marriage intact. After all, he can write his books anywhere.'

'You don't think a wife should be prepared to make a few sacrifices for her husband's sake if he's the bread-winner?'

There was something in his voice that drew her glance to him, although there was little enough to be gleaned from the hazel eyes. 'Are you trying to tell me something?' she asked.

His smile was a disclaimer. 'Just a passing thought.'

'About what you might do if David Barrington decides to stay on?' she hazarded. 'Not much use crossing that particular bridge until you come to it, is it? Anyway, you just told me he said you'd always have a home here.'

'Playing second fiddle? I don't think I could take that,' Gavin swung the car down a narrower side lane in the direction of the sea, a wry twist to the corners of his

mouth. 'You're right, of course, there isn't much point
dwelling on it. Certainly not while the sun's shining and
we have the whole day ahead of us. Hope you brought
plenty of food,' he added. 'Swimming always makes me
hungry.'

'So I've noticed.' She was smiling too, only too willing
to shelve the subject. 'Don't worry, we shan't starve.'

They had the little cove to themselves as usual, and
spent the morning messing around in the water,
swimming out as far as the curving arm of the bay to lie
on the rocks in the sun, until the cool breeze sent them
back in again, exploring the pools which abounded
along the shoreline.

It was going on for one o'clock before they ate, shar-
ing the food Thea had packed with a couple of gulls
who had spotted them from on high. Afterwards, lying
replete on the sand at Gavin's side, Thea gazed up at
the moving white clouds and wondered why she felt so
restless. It took Gavin to put it into words.

'It isn't the same any more, is it?' he said ruefully.
'Not much use telling yourself to put things to the back
of your mind when they refuse to stay there. Dave isn't
going to be easy to get rid of, I can sense that much
now.'

'Dave?' The question was soft.

'It's what he prefers. Suits him better than David, I
have to admit.'

Thea could only agree. David was a gentle name, and
he was far from that. Dave Barrington—the very
thought of him taughtened her nerves. On impulse she
put out her hand and took hold of Gavin's, feeling his
fingers curl about hers.

'Do we have to wait until Christmas to get engaged?'
she asked. 'Let's do it now.'

'Not very practical, considering I didn't bring a ring

with me.' His tone was light but not casual. He rolled over to look at her, lips curved in a smile of regret. 'You know what we agreed. It's best not to rush into things.'

'Only where people aren't sure of their feelings,' she returned. 'We're sure, aren't we?'

There was no hesitation in the reply. 'Of course. It's just—well, we did promise Mother it wouldn't be before Christmas.'

'I was forgetting.' The light had dimmed a little in her eyes. 'I don't really think she wants us to get married, Gavin.'

This time there was hesitation, his eyes not quite meeting hers. 'I suppose,' he said at last, 'she's wondering what kind of future we're going to have as the poor in-laws.'

'That's ridiculous!' Thea declared hotly. 'The money isn't David Barrington's personally. He can only use a proportion of the income for his own needs, and only that while he's actually living at Whirlow. In effect, he's paid a salary by the Estate, the same way you are. A pretty hefty one, I'll admit, but it still doesn't make him a millionaire.'

'I realise that.' The hazel eyes looked drawn. 'And if he decides to manage the place himself, what then? I can hardly draw a salary for doing nothing, and I can't keep a wife on fresh air. I know he said we could always stay on, but you'd no more want to live off his charity than I would.'

'No,' she said, 'I wouldn't.' Her jaw firmed. 'All right, so if the worst comes to the worst you'll have to find another job. With your experience that shouldn't be too difficult.'

Gavin's expression was curious. 'You'd be willing to leave Sculla?'

'If necessary.' She made a small wry gesture. 'I'm not going to pretend I'd want to do it, but it might be the only solution.'

'You could be right.' He sounded thoughtful. 'Mother would be okay. With what Douglas left her plus her own little income, she'd have enough to live independently of any hand-outs. She certainly merits the right to spend the rest of her life at Whirlow, if she wants to.' His glance came back into focus on Thea's face, expression softening. 'You're too good for me, you know that?'

'No, I'm not!' Her tone was fierce, the clutch of her hand on his arm almost equally so. 'I love you, Gavin!'

He kissed her then, his lips warm but not especially urgent. It was one of the things she loved about him, this willingness to wait for the deeper intimacies. If she sometimes wondered a little at her own lack of overriding passion it was a thought she pushed to the back of her mind. What they had was enough for now. The rest would come with time.

They left the cove at three after another swim. Only when they reached the car did Thea ask Gavin if he was going to be able to make tea at her home.

'I don't see why not,' he said. 'Only maybe we should just call back at the house first to see how Mother's coping.'

'I'm not dressed for visiting,' Thea pointed out, glancing down at her brief shorts and top and visualising Mrs Barrington's reaction. 'You know how your mother feels about that.'

Gaving didn't attempt to deny it. 'You can always sit in the car while I have a quick word.'

'All right.' She had no intention of making things difficult for him, even if the thought of waiting outside did go against the grain. Her smile was purely for his benefit. 'Let's go.'

Despite the lack of real distance, it took them almost fifteen minutes to reach the house via the narrow, twisting roads, including the several minutes spent backing up to allow free passage to a tractor from Meadow Farm. Thea had told David Barrington that a couple of cars was no problem, but that wasn't strictly true. There were several on the island who had reason to curse the introduction, especially where it wasn't really needed. On one occasion shortly after Douglas's death, Thea herself had tentatively suggested a return to traditional transport, only to realise that for Gavin there was a certain prestige attached to his use of a car. The subject had not been mentioned again.

Whirlow lay at the end of a curving, gateless driveway—gateless because there was no one who needed to be kept out. Added to over the years, the resulting building had a haphazard charm with its turreted gables and sprawling lines. Too large by far for one family, much of it was closed off, the fine furnishings shrouded in dust sheets. A pity, Thea privately thought, yet could suggest no alternative solution. Under the terms of the trust, the house itself could not be sub-divided.

Gavin left her in the car outside the big oak doors while he went to find his mother. From where she sat, Thea looked down across sloping lawns to the little lake Douglas Barrington's predecessor had caused to be constructed, admiring the sheer beauty of the tall green trees reflected in the still water. No Dutch elm disease here as yet. One could only hope there never would be. Sculla was a world within itself, removed from outside influences in more ways than one. Leaving it would be a wrench, yet if it had to be done she would try to do it, without too much regret. Gavin's future was the most important thing.

She had been sitting there some fifteen minutes before she began to get restless. True, Gavin could hardly nip in and nip straight out again, but she hoped he wasn't going to be much longer. She got out of the car to stretch her legs, leaning against the bonnet to look towards the house with a contemplative eye. Five minutes more and, Mrs Barrington or no Mrs Barrington, she was going to go inside and find out what was keeping him. Giving in to the former's somewhat petty little preferences was probably foolish anyway. What on earth difference did it make what she was wearing, providing she was decently covered? Gavin's mother was not an unpleasant woman, just an indulged one. Perhaps it was high time someone stopped the rot.

She was unaware of David Barrington's approach across the grass from the direction of the stables, and almost jumped out of her skin when he spoke.

'Aren't you allowed in the house?'

He was standing on the far side of the bonnet when she turned, the speculative expression springing once more in the grey eyes as they slid over her skimpy tank top. He was wearing riding breeches and a thin cotton shirt, the sleeves of the latter rolled to reveal muscular forearms. Hairy but not too hairy, Thea noted, in passing. Dark, where Gavin's was so fair, and therefore far more apparent. Something knotted deep inside her.

'I'm allowed,' she said, 'but not approved. Not like this.'

'Janine?' He sounded more amused than anything. 'You look fine to me—but then I'm new around here. I take it Gavin's inside?'

'Yes.' Her chin lifted a fraction. 'He's coming home to tea with me. Mom suggested I invite you too, but I told her you'd hardly be interested.'

Dark brows lifted in the fashion that was already

becoming familiar. 'Do you always decide how people are likely to react?'

'No.' Just for a moment she faltered, then swiftly rallied again. 'Was I wrong?'

'With regard to the interest, very much so. I'd like to meet your parents.'

'You mean you'll come?'

His smile was dry. 'Not today, thanks, I'm tied up. I planned on spending a few hours going through the books.'

'That means you'll need Gavin.'

'Not necessarily. Time enough tomorrow for a detailed accounting. You'll be here then, won't you?'

'Nine o'clock sharp.' For the first time Thea remembered that this man was actually her employer. She wasn't sure whether the reminder had been deliberate or not. She turned in some relief as one of the double doors opened. 'Here's Gavin now.'

The latter came towards them rather slowly, looking from one to the other as if he thought they might have been talking about him.

'Enjoy your ride?' he asked his cousin. 'Mother said you went out more than two hours ago.'

'That's right. I took the Bay—Major, isn't it? Rode over to the village and back up through the woods above one of the farms.'

'Meadow Farm,' Thea supplied. 'The tenant is Rob Colton. The wood is called Springfield.'

'Thanks. Maybe I should have taken you with me.' There was no mockery that she could trace in his tone, but the grey eyes had a certain light about them. 'Tomorrow we'll all three be taking a tour of Whirlow property; I want to see exactly how things are. Hope you enjoy your tea.'

They watched him move away towards the house

before getting into the car. Gavin was the first to speak.

'I've a feeling he's going to be dissatisfied with what he finds on principle.'

'Perhaps not entirely,' Thea came back, trying to be open-minded. 'After all, we both know there's a lot needs doing to make things perfect on Sculla.'

'I tried,' he defended, and Thea put out a swift hand to cover his on the wheel.

'Of course you did. I'm not sure what your stepfather was saving the money for as he couldn't touch it anyway, but he was the one who had to sanction improvements—anyone with any common sense at all realises that. If David Barrington wants to start setting things to rights good luck to him. It can only make your job easier.'

'As long as it lasts.'

'I thought we agreed not to talk about that until we know something concrete.'

'Yes, we did.' Gavin gave her a determined smile. 'Not another word on the subject!'

CHAPTER THREE

MONDAY was cloudy but warm, the glass steady on 'fair'. Dressed carefully in a pleated grey skirt and a fine check blouse, Thea rode her bicycle over to Whirlow for ten minutes to the hour, leaving it parked over in the stable yard while she went in through the side entrance of the house to the office premises.

She was first arrival, but then she expected to be. So far as she could see nothing had been touched, yet she was pretty certain that David Barrington would have kept his word about last night. This was his house, if only for the duration of his life; he had a perfect right to touch anything in it. She had to clamp down on this sense of intrusion.

Gavin came in promptly on the hour, his concealed yawn evidence of a restless night.

'Dave will be along in a minute or two,' he said. 'He's having a word with Mother.'

'Are they getting along all right?' asked Thea.

'They seem to be.' He sounded faintly disgruntled about it. 'She thinks he's got a lot about him. I daresay she's right. From what he was telling us over breakfast, he's led quite a varied life.'

Thea looked at him for a moment. 'Did he volunteer the information?'

'No, Mother asked a lot of questions, that's all.' He put the sheaf of papers he had picked up back on his desk without doing more than glance at the top copy, adding sourly, 'I doubt if he ever volunteers anything.'

'I thought you were beginning to quite like him,' she commented, and drew a defensive shrug.

'If he were anyone else but who he is I might.'

'He can't help being who he is.'

'So?' His glance was sharp. 'Whose side are you on?'

'Yours, of course.' Her tone was placatory. 'It's just that I'm beginning to realise it isn't his fault he got landed with Sculla. Taking everything into consideration, I'd say there's a very good chance he won't want to leave his place in Natal on a permanent basis. Sculla has limitations. He might even feel too constricted after living all his life in a country as big as South Africa.'

'Yes, well, let's hope you're right.' Gavin looked round as the door opened to admit the older man, face taking on a closed look. 'Did you want to get off right away?'

'No point in hanging around.' Dave Barrington's nod to Thea was perfunctory. 'Bring a notebook. From what I saw yesterday, Meadow Farm is in need of roofing repairs for a start.'

It was a long morning, and not an easy one. By midday Thea's notebook was almost half filled and they had only so far visited four of the farmhouses. Dave's comments had grown terser as they progressed, his step-cousin's face tauter. None of the details picked out were the latter's fault, yet he was obviously the one who was going to be blamed. It was a real pity, Thea reflected, that Dave Barrington hadn't known his uncle; it might have made for a better understanding of the situation.

It was a silent ride back to the house for lunch, neither man making any move towards discussing the subject. Only when they were getting out of the car did Dave speak.

'We'll make a start on the village this afternoon,' he said. 'I want the full picture. What about your place, Thea? Any outstanding problems?'

Her name sounded strange on his lips. Studiously she avoided direct confrontation with the grey eyes. 'The best person to ask about that is my father.'

'He's probably the best person to ask about a whole lot of things,' he agreed curtly. 'Will he be available this afternoon?'

She shook her head. 'He took a child across to the mainland for hospital treatment this morning. He won't be back before nine.'

'The same boat we came across in?'

'Yes.'

'I see.' There was decisiveness in the set of his jaw. 'That's one of the first things we're going to have to do something about.'

Mrs Barrington was already seated at the dining room table, her features set in lines of expectancy. At fifty-seven she was still a very good-looking woman, although the white-blonde hair and too heavy make-up tended to harden her.

'So what do you think of our little island?' she asked, ignoring the fact that strictly speaking the word should have been 'your'. 'Charming, isn't it!'

'On the surface,' Dave agreed. 'I'll be able to tell you more after I've seen the rest of it.' To Gavin he added unexpectedly, 'Where does the island water come from?'

'Natural Springs,' the other said.

'Pure?'

'As pure as any you'd get out of a town tap—purer, as it isn't laced with fluoride. No loss suffered either. The visiting dentist swears he's never seen teeth in better condition than here on Sculla.'

There was no reaction to the latter statement. 'How about drought conditions?'

'It's very rarely dry enough for long enough to cause any real problems,' put in Janine Barrington, refusing to be left out of the conversation. 'Something to do with where we're situated, I believe. A nuisance at times, but every cloud has its silver lining.'

The answering smile was polite rather than genuinely amused, but it satisfied Janine. She had come alive in a way which Thea, for one, found somewhat nauseating. David Barrington was not only her nephew by marriage, he was also a good twenty years younger. She wondered if he too had noted the arch quality in his aunt's manner, and come to the conclusion that it wouldn't bother him if he had. It was doubtful, she thought, if any woman had ever bothered him in any lasting sense. His kind walked alone.

Janine carried the conversation throughout the rest of the meal, leaving very little room for anything but the occasional monosyllabic reply on Dave's part, and totally ignoring the fact that others were present at all. In the space of half an hour he learned her complete life history up to the point of coming to Sculla.

'Douglas was such a fine man,' she finished with an air of really meaning it. 'So different from my first husband. Fortunately, Gavin doesn't take after his father at all.'

'I never really knew him,' Gavin admitted without rancour. 'I was only around two years old when he died. Douglas was a more than adequate substitute.'

'Did you always call him by his first name?' Dave asked on a casual note. 'I'd have thought at eight you'd have been young enough to regard him as a father in name as well as substance.'

'It was his own choice.' The younger man's voice had

hardened just a little. 'He wanted me to see him as a friend, not just a substitute father figure.'

It was impossible to read any reaction in the lean features, but Thea could have hazarded a guess that Dave did not agree with the reasoning behind that statement. She felt rather the same way herself. A father could be both friend as well as parent. Her own was a case in point.

Dave showed no inclination to linger over coffee. By two o'clock they were in the car again and heading for the village. The Smithy was the first port of call. Reticent to the point of enmity at first, Tom Crailee unbent enough to present a quite formidable list of complaints once urged to do so.

'Been asking for a new door on the privy for a couple of years,' he growled. 'Rain comes in real bad. Nearly got to the point of paying Col Farrow to make me one myself.'

'How many other places are without an indoor toilet?' asked Dave grimly on the way out.

'Three or four.' Gavin sounded defensive. 'Just the ones that don't have anywhere suitable to put them.'

'Then they'll have to be incorporated—even if it means partial rebuilding. This is the twentieth century, for God's sake!' He stopped at the car, looking along the quiet, sunlit street with an eye that saw beyond the pretty façade. 'We'll walk from here. I've a feeling I haven't seen the worst of it yet.'

Thea caught Gavin's eye as the older man turned away, and very quickly shook her head. Now was not the time to start protesting his own lack of responsibility for the neglect of years. Much of what had been done had been at his instigation, and Dave must be made to realise the position. Only that would come later, when he had all the facts at his finger tips.

If the morning had seemed long, the afternoon seemed infinitely longer. By half past four, when David Barrington decided to call it a day, they were still little more than halfway through. Back at the house, he told Thea he wanted all today's notes typed up before she left so that he could spend the evening reading them through in order to get a better overall picture. In the meantime, he added brusquely to his step-cousin, they had things to discuss.

Thea started on her allotted task the moment they left the room, aware that she could do little to help Gavin weather what was obviously coming. Once the latter had explained it would be appreciated that his hands had been tied by Douglas Barrington's refusal to sanction more than a certain amount of money to be spent on repairs and improvements in any one year. Meadow Farm had needed new tiles on the roof since this last winter's gales, it was true, but the rain wasn't getting in yet, whereas Bob Gifford's place farther along the valley had required instant attention. Dave Barrington was like all new brooms: out for a clean sweep. Well, good luck to him, providing he didn't blame Gavin for not having made it before.

She worked through till six without seeing either of the two men again. Leaving the completed notes on Gavin's desk, she went to look for him, locating him eventually in one of the hothouses talking with the head gardener.

'I thought you'd gone long ago,' he said when they were outside. 'Your hours are nine to five, regardless of what *he* says!'

'I didn't mind staying on,' Thea returned with a swift sideways glance at the set features. 'I gather it didn't go so well?'

'You could call that the understatement of the year.'

He kicked at a pebble lying on the fine gravel path with some force, sending it spinning into a flower bed. 'According to his lights, no estate manager worth his calling just sits back and accepts a lack of funding. Apparently I should have bludgeoned Douglas into releasing the money.'

'That's unfair,' protested Thea hotly. 'He never even met Douglas!'

'He didn't need to. I've a feeling he'd have succeeded where I failed.'

'There's no way of proving that, and I don't believe it anyway. Your stepfather was a fine man in many respects, but stubborn to the point of intractability in some things—we all know that. These last few years he became obsessed with cutting down on expenditure. There was nothing anyone could have done about it. The custodian of the trust has absolute power.'

Gavin's smile was wry. 'I wish you could convince Dave.'

'I'll certainly try,' she said on a sudden surge of determination. 'Where is he?'

Gavin shook his head, smiling despite himself. 'I'd rather you didn't. His kind would have scant respect for a man who let a woman go rooting for him. You wouldn't alter his opinion in any case. In his own way he's as intractable as Douglas was—a family trait, I imagine.'

Thea subsided, aware that he was probably right. She would do little good and possibly some harm by interfering. Gavin had to sort things out for himself. 'What are you going to do?' she asked. 'About the job, I mean.'

'For the moment, nothing.' He sounded resigned. 'He hasn't suggested I should start looking around for something else, and until he does I'm staying put. Maybe once having got things straightened out—including me—he'll see fit to leave me in charge.'

'And you'd stay on those terms?'

'Providing he wasn't here himself. Hardly likely he would be under those circumstances. If he does decide to stay it will be as owner-manager, that I'm sure of.'

Thea was sure too. No half measures for Dave Barrington. She felt torn in two by conflicting loyalties. On the one hand he was obviously going to be good for Sculla with his sweeping policies, yet the way he was treating Gavin could hardly be called fair-minded. The man was a bigot, she decided. Having once made up his mind about something he would not allow himself to be deflected from that opinion. There was something oddly disturbing in that reflection.

It was gone half past six by the time she got home. Her mother had supper ready and waiting, together with a great many questions regarding the news which had already circumnavigated the village.

'They're saying he plans on pulling down just about every house and cottage on Main Street and starting over,' she said on a concerned note. 'That's not really true, is it?'

'No, of course not,' Thea assured her. 'He was pretty scathing about the general condition of some of them, but they're all matters that can be taken in hand reasonably simply. I doubt if anyone is going to have to move out lock, stock and barrel. If you and Dad can list any repairs or major improvements needed here it will save some time tomorrow. He hasn't nearly finished assessing the situation yet.'

'Well, it's certainly not before time that somebody did put things to rights,' Margaret agreed. 'I know Gavin did his best for everybody, but he couldn't work miracles. I suppose we should thank heaven that the electricity cable was laid across before Douglas came into power or we might still be using oil lamps and wood fires!' She paused before adding curiously, 'How is Gavin getting along with his step-cousin?'

'He isn't,' Thea admitted. 'Dave seems to think he's to blame for what Douglas wouldn't let him do.'

'Dave?' Her mother's eyebrows had lifted. 'Did he ask you to call him that?'

'No, but Gavin calls him that and it rubs off.' Thea refused to meet the other's gaze. 'Don't worry, I wouldn't dream of being so familiar to his face.'

'So Gavin doesn't care for being the scapegoat,' Margaret persisted, abandoning the other subject. 'It doesn't sound too good a working relationship.'

Thea's shrug held a philosophical acceptance. 'No—well, we'll just have to wait and see.'

It was too fine an evening to remain indoors. After supper she changed into jeans and a sweater and went round the corner to the field where Lady Luck had her summer quarters, happy as always in the knowledge that the mare was hers, bought and kept out of her own earnings.

As she saddled up, it occurred to her for the first time that Lady would be one more loss if it came about that Gavin had to make that move in the end. Not an irreconcilable one, of course, but a wrench nevertheless.

'Still,' she murmured softly to the animal as she swung herself up, 'it hasn't happened yet, and maybe never will. I've got to stop crossing bridges before I come to them.'

Because of the balmy evening she rode out farther than she had intended, returning well after nine to rub the animal down before turning her loose to graze. Tired but content, she made her way homeward with the saddle draped across her arm, the latter emotion turning to surprise at the sight of the car parked outside the front gate. It was unlike Gavin to turn up out of the blue like this, and they had certainly made no arrangements to see each other this evening. Something had to be wrong, she thought in quick concern, hurrying her footsteps.

'We're in here, dear,' called Margaret Ralston from the little front living room as Thea entered the house. 'Bring yourself a cup if you want some coffee.'

Thea dropped the heavy saddle thankfully to the floor in a corner of the hall and pushed back a tendril of hair from her forehead, unaware of the streak of dust she left in its place. Dave Barrington was seated at her mother's side on the faded chintz sofa under the leaded window, one knee lifted across the other in an attitude of total relaxation. Her father sat opposite in his favourite if all too rarely used chair, the glass of whisky in his hand matching the one at present resting on the low table in front of the younger man.

'Mr Barrington was down by the harbour when the *Molly* docked,' explained Margaret, 'so he gave your father a lift home.'

'Killing two birds with one stone,' the former rejoined easily. 'And I asked you to make it Dave.' The grey eyes had not left Thea's face except for one brief excursion downwards over her jean-clad figure. 'I hear you keep your own pony.'

'Horse,' she corrected. 'Lady is over fifteen hands.' She didn't move from the doorway, conscious of her faint horsy aroma. 'What did you mean by "killing two birds with one stone"?'

'Quite simple. I wanted to talk with your father, and it seemed a good opportunity.' His smile was for the other man. 'I've learned a whole lot about Sculla tonight. Nobody knows a place and its people like the local G.P.'

'It's good to know there's somebody concerned enough to ask,' returned John Ralston warmly. 'Your uncle had his good points, but he turned a blind eye where it suited.'

'So I understood from Gavin.'

'Except that from him you didn't believe it,' put in Thea on impulse, and drew the grey eyes back to her.

'It didn't take him long to get that off his chest.' There was irony in the comment. 'I hope you were ready to offer proper comfort.'

'It was obvious what you were thinking,' she defended, already regretting the too hasty remark. 'Gavin didn't need to tell me anything!'

'A mind-reader too!' This time he was looking at her mother, one brow quirked in amusement. 'That's an accomplished daughter you have.'

'But not a very respectful one,' came the wry re-joinder. 'Thea, you shouldn't speak to Mr—Dave like that. After all, he is your employer.'

'Oh, come on! Those days are surely long gone.' Dave was smiling as he said it, but there was a certain glint in his eyes visible to Thea if to no one else. 'Plain speaking was always preferable to a stab in the back.'

'*Did* you want some coffee?' asked Margaret hastily, obviously fearing what her daughter might say next.

Thea shook her head. 'I'm going up for a bath.'

'Walk down to the gate with me first,' invited Dave. 'There's a couple of things I'd like to discuss.' He lifted the whisky glass, drained the remainder of the contents at a swallow and put it down again as he came to his feet. 'Thanks for the hospitality, Mrs Ralston—Doctor. I'll see to it that those jobs are taken care of.'

'No preferential treatment, if you don't mind,' said the latter humorously. 'I'd hate it to be thought we were jumping any queues.'

Thea led the way outside in silence, vitally aware of the tall strength of him at her back.

'I see you've taken over the car,' she commented on reaching the gate.

'Not taken over just utilised,' Dave corrected as she swung it open to let him through. 'Difficult to offer a lift on horseback.'

With the wood between them she felt safer, though from what she wasn't all that sure. 'You mean you went down purposely to meet Dad?'

'In a word, yes. Seemed a better idea than doing it formally.' The pause was brief. 'I like your parents.'

'So do I.' She said it stiffly. 'Is that all you wanted to talk about?'

'No.' His voice had hardened a fraction. 'There's a small matter of conflicting interests to be taken care of.'

Thea gazed at him, willing herself to show no reaction. 'I'm not sure I understand.'

'You understand perfectly. Resented I might be, but I'm here and, for the present at least, I'm staying. If you want to go on working for the Estate, you're going to have to reconcile yourself to that fact.' He had half turned away to the car before apparently recollecting something else he wished to say, looking back at her in the dusk. 'Incidentally, I'm sending Gavin to the mainland for a few days. I can't promise he'll be back for the weekend.'

'That's all right,' she said. 'Gavin and I can be together anytime. One weekend isn't going to hurt us.'

'That's reassuring.' He opened a door and slid behind the wheel, switching on the ignition as he did so. He didn't look in her direction again.

John Ralston was coming out from the living room as Thea went back indoors.

'How's young Paul?' she asked, remembering the reason for his trip to the mainland. 'Did you see him settled?'

'Yes, and he seemed reasonably happy, considering. We shan't be any nearer knowing what's wrong with him for a couple of days yet, but they're going to keep me advised of his progress.' His tone altered. 'I'm impressed with your new boss. He's a real man of action.'

'Yes, isn't he?' Her own voice was toneless. 'We're not going to know ourselves by the time he's through with us.' She gave her father a bright little smile. 'I'm going up for that bath and an early night. It's been a long day.'

Gavin left on the Thursday morning, his mission to secure the services of a reliable building firm willing and able to put men on Sculla for a period of time sufficient to cover all necessary repairs and renovation work.

'Dave wants comparative estimates from at least four firms based on the work sheets we drew up,' he told Thea before sailing on the *Molly*. 'It's going to take time.'

'Why couldn't he simply ring round a few?' she demanded, knowing she was being unreasonable even as she said it.

Gavin's smile and shrug confirmed it. 'It isn't the kind of job you can describe over a telephone, and there aren't going to be many willing to send out a man to assess the situation without some prior knowledge of what might be entailed. You'll be working directly with Dave while I'm gone. Think you're going to be able to stand it?'

'With an effort,' she said, and tried to ignore the faint

sense of panic deep down inside her. She reached up to kiss him, clinging to him for a moment as if half afraid to let him out of her sight. 'Take care.'

She watched the *Molly* out of the harbour before turning back to where she had left her bicycle leaning up against the wall, thankful for the fine weather. Gavin was no great sailor at the best of times. When it came right down to it they didn't really have so much in common at all, she mused, pushing the cycle up the incline. It just went to show that love took little heed of extraneous detail.

She was at the house by twenty-five to nine, forced to retrace her steps round to the front when she found the side entrance still locked. Dave came out from the breakfast room as she entered the hallway.

'You're early,' he greeted her. 'I was just about to phone through and tell you not to bother coming in this morning. I think we both deserve a little time off after these last few days.'

How about Gavin? she wanted to ask, but refrained. 'I have plenty to do,' she said instead. 'And I'd rather be working than sitting twiddling my thumbs at home.'

'No need for that either. I'm going up to change for riding. Why don't you go on home and do the same? There's a lot of the island I haven't had chance to see yet.'

Thea looked at him for a long moment without speaking, taking in his dark attraction with that same faint sense of trepidation. 'Are you asking me to come with you?' she queried at length, and saw the firm mouth take on a slant.

'Is that so strange? You know the place—I don't. Of course, if you object——'

'I don't.' The denial came of its own accord, too fast for her liking. She made some attempt to mitigate any.

possible impression. 'I love riding any time.'

'Then that's settled. You cut on back now and I'll pick you up in half an hour or so. That time enough?'

'Plenty.' Her smile was involuntary. 'It will make a change from sitting in the office.'

Mrs Ralston was out shopping when Thea reached the house, her father still in surgery. She changed swiftly into clean jeans and a fine checked shirt, briefly regretting her lack of proper riding gear. The boots and hat she had purchased from Mrs Templeton, but the rest of the latter's expensive outfit had not been the right size. Her next shopping expedition to the mainland must include at least a pair of jodhpurs, she decided now. There were none to be bought here on Sculla. Those who rode horseback at all scarcely worried about appearances.

Dave arrived while she was still in the process of saddling Lady. He was riding the big bay gelding again.

'That's a fine animal,' he observed without getting down. 'She must have cost a packet.'

'I got her for a song,' Thea admitted, tightening the girths. 'The wife of a writer who lived here for a time last year sold her to me when they left.'

'She must have taken a liking to you.'

'Yes, I think she did.' It was a simple statement of fact. 'I would have paid more, but she wouldn't take it. She just wanted Lady to have a good home.'

'Lucky Lady.' His tone was light. 'Do you want a leg-up?'

'I can manage, thanks.' Thea suited her actions to her words, hoisting herself lithely into the saddle. 'I never had a chance to get accustomed to having someone help me.'

'Nice to be independent,' he commented with just a faint edge of irony. 'Doesn't Gavin ride?'

'Not from choice. He's none too keen on horses at

all. That's why he likes having the car around.'

'In which case we'll have to make sure to keep it.'

She gave him an oblique glance. 'If he stays.'

'Is there any doubt?' He sounded more curious than surprised. 'Sculla is his home, I already told him that.'

Thea was already sorry she had spoken. What Gavin had told her he had told her in confidence. Having started it, however, she felt bound to continue.

'He took your criticisms rather personally. Isn't that the way they were intended?'

'Not to the extent of making him start looking around for another job. I hadn't realised he was quite that sensitive.'

She flushed, sensing the sardonic quality behind the words. 'I'm giving you the wrong impression. He isn't over-sensitive, just conscious of his position here. Any man would be.'

Dave moved the bay in alongside her as they made their way across the field to the gate on the far side, fleshless brown hands supple on the reins. Outlined against the clear blue of the sky, his profile looked chiselled in stone.

'Most men prefer to fight their own battles,' he said. 'Would Gavin thank you for speaking up for him?'

'No,' she admitted. 'In fact, he asked me not to.'

'Then don't you think you should respect his wishes?' The look he gave her was devoid of humour. 'You can't spend your life smoothing paths, Thea. Let him stand on his own feet.'

He didn't wait for any answer, urging Major on ahead in order to open the gate. Following, Thea bit her lip. She had asked for that. And he was right, of course; she had to stay out of it.

They rode up through Springfield Wood on to the downs above Meadow Farm, putting both animals into a gallop as soon as the terrain allowed for it. On a day like this it was possible to see both east and west coasts from this vantage point. Reining in at the end of the level stretch, Thea sat looking out to sea, temporarily forgetting the man coming up at her back.

'Penny for them,' Dave said lightly after a moment or two. He was sitting with one ankle propped comfortably across the saddle in front of him—a position made even more dangerous by the fact that he wore no headgear. 'Or are they purely private?'

She shook her head, suddenly self-conscious. 'I was thinking how much I love this place, and how I'd hate to leave it.'

There was no immediate answer. He appeared to be considering. 'It isn't always possible to stay the way we are,' he said at length. 'Circumstances change—people change. A small island isn't always going to be enough for you. A place to come back to maybe, on occasion.'

'It's been enough for most of the people I know,' she pointed out.

'Most of the people you know are of a different generation.'

'Gavin isn't.'

His smile was dry. 'Gavin likes playing the country squire. Not much opportunity left for that in England these days, I imagine. You've become insular, the whole lot of you.'

'Including my father?'

'To a certain extent. He sees everything in relationship to Sculla. World events don't particularly interest him.'

'Why should they, unless and until they start to affect us?'

'That's what I mean by insularity.' He studied her windswept hair and fine-skinned features with an odd expression in his eyes. 'Take yourself, for instance. How many other men have you known besides Gavin?'

'Any number,' she defended. 'I went to a mixed college, and he isn't the only man on the island.'

'I meant intimately.'

She was unable to stop the warmth from rising under
her skin. 'Is that any of your business?'

'Not really,' he agreed. 'But it's an interesting
thought. You should have played the field a little before
settling for any one man. That way you'd know you
were getting the best of the bunch.'

'So far as I'm concerned,' she retorted sharply, 'Gavin
is the best of the bunch!'

'Speaking from a limited experience.'

'So what of it?' She was angry, but in control of herself. 'I don't need to read through a whole library to
recognise a good book!'

'Hardly an adequate comparison. Nobody's doubting
Gavin's worthiness.'

'Good, then can we please forget the whole subject?'
She pulled sharply on the mare's rein to turn her, causing the chestnut head to jerk in protest.

'If I got across you take it out on me, not a dumb
animal,' Dave suggested on a caustic note. 'I can hit
back.'

Thea made herself look at him, taking in the spark in
the grey eyes with a sense of confusion. 'Why are you
being like this?' she asked, trying for a direct approach.
'What is it about me that annoys you so much?'

'Your damned complacency, for one thing,' he
returned. 'You're so certain of everything. I'd like to
shake you out of it.'

'Well, you won't,' she stated flatly. 'I know my own
mind, *Mr* Barrington, and neither you nor anyone else
is going to change it for me!'

She was halfway down the slope before she heard him

coming after her, and even then it didn't occur to her that she was being chased with intent until she turned her head and saw his expression. The crooked little smile was a threat in itself, invoking a sensation more akin to exhilaration than fear. She spurred Lady on, ignoring the lack of sense in taking a gradient this steep at a fast canter. If Dave could do it so could she. Let him catch her if he could!

They were on the flat before he did draw level, leaning down from the saddle to take hold of the mare's rein close up by the bit and pull both animals to a standstill. Still holding on, he brought her round in front of his own horse so that he could dismount, slapping Major on the rump in order to send him clear the moment his feet touched the ground. There was a purposeful light in the grey eyes when he looked up at Thea.

'Come on down.'

She made no move to obey, her heart thudding against her ribcage. What he had in mind she wasn't at all certain, but whatever it was she didn't want to know. 'Joke over,' she said. 'Isn't it time we were getting back?'

His answer was swift and sure, one hand reaching up to grasp the back of her belt, the other waiting to catch her as he pulled her bodily out of the saddle. Then she was in his arms and his mouth was on hers.

There was irony in his expression when he finally lifted his head. 'Not quite so sure of yourself after all,' he said. 'You enjoyed that as much as I did.'

Thea could hardly deny it. The kiss had been expertly given. She could still feel the warm pressure against her lips, the tantalising movement drawing her on to respond in kind.

'You took me by surprise,' she got out with creditable steadiness.

'Meaning you'd have reacted quite differently with prior warning?' The glint became a gleam, hard and derisive. 'So this time you know what's coming——'

'Don't!' She put both hands flat against his broad chest, pushing him away with a strength that surprised them both. 'All right, so I enjoyed it. Wasn't that the idea?'

'Of course.' He was watching her with sardonic amusement, making no attempt to let her go. 'What are you afraid of?'

'I'm not afraid.' She forced herself to look at him directly in the eyes without flinching. 'I just don't see any point in repeating the experiment. Gavin may lack some of your expertise, but at least I don't have to think about all the girls he would have to have kissed to acquire it!'

'Ouch,' he said softly. 'That was below the belt.'

'You asked for it.'

'I guess I did at that.' He let his hands fall away from her, stepping back to allow her freedom to move out from the mare's flank. His gaze held a different sort of assessment this time. 'You're quite a girl, Thea.'

'Thanks.' She did her best to sound unmoved. 'Coming from you I'm not sure that's a compliment.'

The smile had a certain dryness about it. 'I'm not sure it is either. Can we get lunch at the Big Tree?'

Thea nodded, taken aback by the sudden change of direction. 'It's barely eleven,' she felt bound to add.

'So we'll take the long way round.'

She stayed where she was as he took hold of the gelding's reins, watching the play of muscle through the thin material of his shirt when he hoisted himself into the saddle. It was hard to believe that only a few short moments ago she had been in his arms, feeling that same breadth of shoulder beneath her fingers, the hard strength of his body crushing the breath from her own. Just one kiss given without any kind of emotional commitment, yet it had awoken something in her that Gavin's kisses rarely touched.

It mustn't happen again, she thought a little desperately. Whatever it took, it mustn't happen again!

CHAPTER FOUR

THE Big Tree was opposite the church gates. Built of stone brought across from the mainland over a hundred years before, the latter had seen several vicars come and go, with the present incumbent still a relative newcomer. He was seated outside the pub talking to Tom Crailee when Thea and Dave rode up.

'Been showing Mr Barrington something of the island, have you?' he remarked as they dismounted to tether the animals to the railing close by. 'Nice day for it.' He waited until they were closer before adding unabashedly, 'You wouldn't like to try persuading our friend to join our little flock on Sunday, would you, Thea? So far I've failed miserably.'

'I'm hardly the one to try persuading anybody,' she returned in some discomfiture, 'considering I'm not always there myself.'

'I had noticed.' The tone was bland. 'One hour a week isn't so very much to ask. If you set the example, Mr Barrington might follow.'

'I doubt it.' Dave sounded amicable enough about it, but there was no doubting his word. 'Weddings and funerals—and only those when pressed.'

'You can't blame a man for making the attempt,' came the comfortable response. 'Your uncle was the mainstay of the congregation—never missed a single service in five years.'

'Good for him.' Dave nodded his head at the almost empty glasses on the table in front of the two men. 'How about a refill?'

'Not for me, thanks,' said the vicar. 'One half pint a day is my limit.'

'And it's time I was getting back across.' Tom was on his feet as he spoke, the movement light for a man of his size. 'See you're riding Major,' he added to Dave. 'Might be an idea if I took a look at his shoes while you're down. Been some time since he had a new set.'

'He hasn't been ridden a great deal,' Dave answered, 'but help yourself. I'll pick him up when we finish lunch.'

'Speaking of which, I'd better be getting along for mine, or it will be burnt offerings again.' The Reverend Mr Conniston hoisted his own not inconsiderable bulk from the bench, pausing to flick a dandelion clock from the sleeve of the tweed jacket beneath which he wore the collar and vest of his calling. 'I hear Gavin went to the mainland.'

Thea nodded, wondering if her guilt showed in her face. One thing was certain, Gavin would not have spent the morning kissing another girl. She could feel Dave's presence at her side as tangibly as if he were touching her still.

'That's the wedding the whole island is looking forward to,' continued the clergyman. 'They make a fine couple, wouldn't you say, Mr Barrington?'

'Oh, very.' The irony was barely distinguishable. 'When's the wedding to be?'

'No date set as yet. What do you say, Thea?'

'We don't plan on getting engaged until Christmas,' she murmured uncomfortably. 'Probably next spring.'

Dave's shrug was easy. 'Preferable to jumping in with both feet, I suppose.'

'We take things slowly on Sculla,' the other man agreed. 'Don't forget about Sunday, Thea. Your mother would be delighted to have you with her.'

'I'd say you were committed,' Dave observed with some malice as they went on into the building. 'Is Gavin a churchgoer?'

'He used to go regularly with his stepfather,' she said. 'Not so much now. We usually spend Sundays at the beach when it's fine.'

'Something else I've yet to sample. Maybe I should take Gavin's place this Sunday.'

The little lounge bar was empty of customers, giving Thea pause in the doorway. 'We'd better go through to the saloon,' she said, choosing not to pursue the offer. 'There's no one serving in here.'

'There soon can be.' Dave indicated a nearby table. 'Sit down while I go and find what's on the menu.'

'I can tell you that,' she said. 'It's always the same. Ploughman's, or steak and kidney pie with peas. They're home-made, though.'

'Sounds good enough. Two pies, then.'

He had gone before she could say yes or no, leaving her to sink to a seat on the padded bench set into a window embrasure and await his return. She didn't want to be alone with him, she acknowledged. Not after this morning. Their whole relationship had changed from the moment when he had kissed her, and not for the better. She was attracted to him, she was bound to admit that much. He was like no other man she had ever met before, and she didn't know how to handle the situation. She wished he had never come to Sculla at all; everything had been fine till then.

Dave was back in what seemed a ridiculously short time bearing a tray with two steaming plates on it.

'Just came in at the right moment,' he said. 'They're fresh out of the oven.' He put both plates on the table along with cutlery, stacking the tray against a chair leg before sitting down opposite Thea. 'I ordered drinks brought through. Cider okay for you?'

'Fine, thanks.' She had already determined to forget about the incident. It hadn't meant anything, just a momentary impulse on Dave's part—perhaps because there was little other entertainment around. If deep down at the back of her mind the memory refused to be dismissed with quite such ease she was not about to acknowledge the fact, even to herself.

She was grateful when he began to talk about the Estate. This was ground she knew, ground on which she felt sure of herself and her answers. The cider helped too when it came. It was made right here on the island, though not in quantities sufficient for real commercialism. Thea rarely drank it because it was so potent, but she loved its rich, raw taste.

Laughingly she declined a second glass when it was proffered. 'One more of these and you'd have to tie me in the saddle,' she declared. 'I feel lightheaded enough already!'

'It won't do you any harm.' Dave studied her for a moment, a faint curve to his lips. 'You can walk Lady home from here if the worst comes to the worst. I'll take the short cut.'

'You're quite sure you don't need me for anything this afternoon?' she insisted, and saw the smile widen a fraction.

'Nothing that can't wait. Enjoy the rest of the day, and turn up bright and early in the morning—that's all I ask.' He pushed back his chair and got up, reaching in the rear pocket of his breeches. 'I'll go and settle the bill. Don't bother hanging around.'

'All right.' She rose too, oddly reluctant for the moment to pass. 'Thanks for the lunch.'

'Thanks for the company,' he returned equably. 'See you tomorrow.'

It was still only a little after two when Thea reached home after putting Lady out to grass. Her mother was weeding in the front garden, humming cheerfully as she worked.

'I saw your saddle was gone,' she said when Thea told her where she had been. 'I wasn't sure what to think. It was kind of Mr Barrington to give you the day off.'

'He told you to call him Dave,' Thea reminded her. 'Anyway, I've a feeling it was just an excuse to take it off himself. There was plenty we could both have been doing.'

'Well, what's the use of being the boss if you can't put things off when you feel like it?' Margaret Ralston looked back at the flower bed she was tending. 'If you don't have any other plans, perhaps you might like to help me with this. That rain yesterday brought the weeds up in droves!'

Gavin phoned through at seven. It was raining in Truro, he said, and he was feeling more than a little lonely and miserable. How had her day been?

Thea refrained from mentioning the morning ride at all, telling herself it was hardly diplomatic to admit having taken a day off while he was forcibly employed. She would speak of it casually after he got back some time. It was going to be a long weekend, she agreed. Far better if Dave had been willing to leave things over until the Monday when there would have been a clear week in which to get the job done. This way it was going to be Tuesday or even Wednesday before Gavin could get back to Sculla.

Apart from a brief period in the morning, and then again over lunch, she saw nothing of Dave on the Friday. At one point she found herself wondering if he could be deliberately avoiding her, then dismissed the idea as lending too great an importance to a minor incident. In all probability he had already forgotten all about yesterday's little episode. If she had any sense she would do the same.

Saturday was a busy day for the female members of the Ralston family as it was their turn to help provide refreshments for the evening social event. Sold at a set price per plate, along with a choice of tea or coffee, any profit would go to swell the Midsummer Day Festival fund. Thea didn't mind being roped in to help out. Once Lady had been exercised there was little enough to occupy her mind. For perhaps the first time in her life she actually found a day dragging.

The social was held in the school hall, which was the only place big enough to accommodate a hundred and fifty or more people. Each Saturday, volunteers went over to move all the chairs back against the walls and hang a few streamers and balloons to make the place look a little more festive, staying behind afterwards to reverse the process ready for Monday morning. Everyone apart from the very old and the very young attended the weekly event. Four of the island men had formed a group to augment the record player for dancing. With a whist drive going on in one of the classrooms and a bingo session in another, there was something for everyone of reasonably simple tastes.

If she had thought about it at all, Thea had not anticipated that Dave Barrington might put in an appearance at such an unsophisticated affair. Looking up from her coffee urn around nine-thirty to see him standing in the hall doorway brought a surprise closer to shock. He was dressed smartly but casually in fawn slacks and toning shirt open at the throat, and looked completely at ease.

From initial resentment the general consensus of

opinion regarding the new owner had undergone a radical change these last few days. No man as ready to take time and trouble to discover their needs could be all bad, the islanders had reasoned. Foreigner or not, he deserved a chance to prove himself a man of his word.

If he was gratified by the greetings offered from every side he obviously wasn't about to let it go to his head. He chatted civilly with several people in his progression up the room, arriving eventually at the refreshment trestle with a humorous quirk of one dark eyebrow in Thea's direction.

'Coffee, please,' he requested, diving a hand into a pocket for some change. 'How much is that?'

'For Mr Barrington I think it should be on the house,' said the vicar jovially, coming up behind him. 'How about a cup-cake to go with it? I believe Thea made them herself.'

'In which case I can hardly refuse.' Grey eyes sought green, expression amused. 'I shouldn't have thought cooking was one of your major interests.'

'Not cooking,' she corrected. 'Baking. And it isn't. My efforts don't always turn out as well as this.'

He tasted before nodding approval. 'Very good. The coffee's fine too.'

'They're about to start the dancing again,' put in the vicar. 'If you'd like to take a turn or two I'm sure Thea would oblige.'

'Perhaps Mr Barrington would prefer to choose his own partner,' said Thea swiftly, wishing Mr Conniston would stop trying to organise people. 'There's Sally Anders over there, for one. The little blonde,' she added helpfully to Dave.

He didn't even bother to turn his head in the direction indicated. 'I'm happy enough with the first offer. How about it? Can you leave that for a few minutes?'

'I'll take over,' offered Thea's mother, moving down from the sandwiches. 'Most people have finished anyway.' Her smile was for Dave. 'Nice of you to come. People will appreciate it.'

Hands suddenly a little damp, Thea took off her apron and draped it over the back of a nearby chair, sorry now that she hadn't worn something more becoming than the blue cotton skirt and blouse. The group was playing a waltz at present. She only wished it were one of the modern beat numbers where two people could dance without touching.

'Relax,' he murmured softly as they took to the floor. 'I'm not going to bite.'

'That's a relief.' The retort was weak and she knew it, but she felt totally tongue-tied. She searched her mind almost feverishly for something to add, feeling the warmth of his hand at her centre back. 'Why didn't you say you were coming tonight?'

'Because I only decided after dinner,' he returned. 'I thought Janine might come along too, but she didn't feel like it.'

'Mrs Barrington doesn't really care for this sort of thing,' Thea agreed. 'She and your uncle used to put in the occasional appearance for the look of it, that's all.'

'I'm not all that sure what keeps a woman of Janine's type on the island,' Dave admitted. 'She isn't old enough to have settled for a quiet decline.'

Thea could have told him the answer. As long as there was a chance of Gavin taking control of Sculla she would hang on. Only if Dave himself decided to stay on might she consider another course of action, and which form that might take was anyone's guess.

The waltz was followed immediately by a quickstep, and then the Gay Gordons, both of which Dave insisted on doing, although he was not familiar with the latter.

'The club in Colesburg puts on similar affairs to this,' he said when, hot and laughing, the dancers finally came to a halt. 'Maybe just a little more elaborate, perhaps, but in essence there isn't a lot of difference. South African townships generally stay small and fairly simple. If we want a greater variety of entertainment we go down to Durban.'

'Are you missing it?' asked Thea, sensing a certain something in his tone.

His shrug was casual. 'I've barely been away from it long enough.' With one hand he eased the collar of his shirt, running a finger round the back of his neck with a wry grimace. 'It's warm in here. Let's go and find some air.'

Eyes watched the two of them as they made their way to the door, but Thea was in no mood to care. Being with Dave had made this evening special in a way she didn't want to plumb too deeply. She didn't want it to end.

The night was clear, the stars bright. From outside the schoolhouse the sound of music was muted. Scent from the laden orange blossom tree at the side of the iron gateway rose in waves as the air moved gently.

'If only we could have weather like this all summer,' sighed Thea when Dave made no attempt to break the silence. 'It could be snowing tomorrow!'

'Don't exaggerate,' he told her mildly enough. 'I doubt if it ever snows in winter this far south. Anyway,' he added before she could make any reply, 'I didn't bring you out here to talk about the weather.'

She was silent, not quite sure enough of herself to ask the obvious question. It was left to Dave to continue, leaning against a gatepost in a casual stance with one foot lifted across to the bottom rung of the open gate, effectively blocking any line of retreat on her part.

'Tell me,' he said, 'if you didn't work for Whirlow what else would you do here on Sculla?'

'Not a lot,' she admitted. 'There isn't a great deal I could do. That's the main reason why so many of the younger element go to the mainland.'

'So without your job you'd have been doing the same—unless your parents had been willing and able to keep you.'

'I wouldn't have expected them to.' She was puzzled and more than a little alarmed by the turn the conversation appeared to be taking. 'Are you trying to tell me something?'

His expression was hard to gauge in the moonlight. 'Just a hypothetical question.'

'Oh.' Thea was relieved and not bothering to conceal it. 'For a moment I thought you were going to say I wasn't needed any more.'

'Considering the amount of paper work that's going to be coming along in connection with the rebuilding programme, I could hardly be thinking along those lines,' he came back dryly. 'Not that it mightn't be doing you a kindness in the long run to find someone else to take over from you for a period. A year or so living on the mainland would give you a new perspective.'

'I already tried it,' Thea pointed out. 'I had two years at college, to say nothing of school.'

'Living en masse.'

'Not all the time. It wasn't a boarding school I was at. During the week I stayed with a sister of Dad's in Exeter, and just came back here for weekends and holidays.'

'You were still dependent on others. What you really need is a spell entirely on your own—maybe in London. With your abilities it shouldn't be too difficult to find a good job.'

It was a moment or two before she could bring herself to answer, voice a little tauter. 'I don't really think it's up to you to tell me what I need.'

'Maybe not.' He sounded unmoved. 'But somebody should. How can you possibly know what you want from life when you've never experienced any? If you marry Gavin you'll be facing a lot of years together. At least, that's the way it's supposed to go. Do you see yourself growing old alongside him?'

'How can anyone look that far ahead?' she demanded. 'You said it yourself. People change. It has to be taken on trust that the changes are going to be for the better, not worse.'

'He isn't right for you,' Dave insisted. 'Neither are you right for him.'

'I disagree.' She was trembling, partly with anger, partly from some other emotion as yet ill-defined. 'There's never been anyone else for either of us, not on any serious footing. There never could be.'

'If you were really so sure of that you wouldn't be out here with me now,' he rejoined on a soft note. 'Especially after the other morning.'

'That meant no more to me than it did to you.' Her voice was low, but luckily it was steady. 'If I'd protested you'd have taken it as an excuse to carry on.'

'The way I'm doing now?' He reached out a hand and drew her to him, bringing down his foot so that he stood rock-hard against the post. His other hand circled her nape beneath the short tendrils of hair, his touch gentle yet purposeful too. 'I'm not going to let you drift into marriage with my step-cousin,' he declared. 'Not without at least providing a basis for comparison.'

'Dave, don't.' It was less a demand than a plea, her body tensed to the feel of the lean fingers. 'I'm not equipped to play your kind of games.'

'Then it's time you learned, even if only in self-defence.'

The kiss began at the point of her jaw just below her ear, his lips soft and light against her skin. Thea closed her eyes as he moved them slowly downwards towards her mouth, refusing even now to struggle and fight him. She had known deep down that this was likely to happen again, yet she had still consented to come out here with him. Whatever she got from him she merited.

It took every ounce of control she had to stop herself from responding to him when he did find her mouth. Only when he slid a hand down to the curve of her breast did she react involuntarily, grasping the hard, sinewy wrist to stay the movement.

'That's far enough,' she got out.

'Is it?' His voice was still low but with a harder inflection. 'I'm not a fool, Thea. I can feel what's right there in you. You're so repressed it's unbelievable. Doesn't Gavin make love to you at all?'

'I won't discuss him with you,' she responded fiercely.

'You don't need to. You already answered the question. Did it ever occur to you that a man who doesn't want a woman physically might not really want her at all?'

She kept a grip on herself with an effort. 'Then why would he ask me to marry him?'

'Because in his own way he's probably as repressed as you are. You were there, you were available, and you're decidedly easy on the eye. You realise his mother doesn't fully approve?'

'Only since——' She broke off, biting her lip. 'It isn't her place to question his choice.'

'Only since she discovered there was an heir to the Estate,' he finished for her, ignoring the last. 'You knew.

How come she and Gavin didn't?'

'Gavin did,' she said. 'He was the one who told me. He kept it from his mother for the same reason your uncle did—they didn't want her worrying about the future.'

Dave was quiet for a moment, considering. 'A pity they didn't have a child of their own,' he said at length. 'That would have left me right out of the whole affair. On the other hand, Gavin would still have been in the same position.'

'Not quite. A half-brother might have held a different regard for him.' She tested the strength of his hold on her, desisting at once when his grip tightened. 'I want to go back. People will be wondering where we are.'

'We'll go back,' he said, 'after you start being honest with yourself. You're not sure about your feelings for Gavin, are you?' The hands on her shoulders hardened still further when she failed to reply. '*Are* you?'

'Thea?' It was Margaret Ralston calling from the direction of the main doors. 'They're waiting for you to draw the raffle!'

Where they were standing was fortunately out of sight of the school building. Dave let her go, eyes steely in the moonlight. 'I haven't finished with you yet,' he promised. 'Not by a long chalk. We're going to find the real Thea Ralston, you and I.'

She ignored him, stepping through the gateway to lift an acknowledging hand to the figure standing outside the double doors. 'Coming!'

Dave caught her up before she was more than a couple of steps across the yard, strolling at her side with hands thrust casually into the pockets of his slacks.

'Sorry for keeping her so long,' he apologised easily when they reached the spot where Margaret still waited. 'We were discussing Estate affairs.'

'Oh, I see.' The relief was faint but unmistakable. 'Are you coming in again?'

'I don't think so. I told Janine I'd only be gone an hour or so—with Gavin away she finds the evenings lonely.' He gave them both a brief salute. 'Goodnight.'

Margaret said nothing until they were inside the building and treading the corridor down to the hall.

'You shouldn't really have gone outside with Dave,' she stated mildly. 'At least, you shouldn't have stayed out quite so long. You know how people talk.'

'Only because they've nothing else to think about,' Thea retorted with unwonted sharpness, and was at once contrite. 'I'm sorry,' she tagged on swiftly. 'That was uncalled-for. Who decided I should draw the raffle this week?'

'The Vicar, I think.'

Someone else concerned for her welfare, reflected Thea with unaccustomed irony. If he hadn't been quite so ready to push her on to Dave none of the last fifteen minutes might have happened at all. And on the other hand, the better side of her responded, if she hadn't been quite so ready to accept that invitation to go out-side it wouldn't have happened for certain.

She slept badly that night, getting up at seven to a morning misty with the promise of heat to come.

'Make the most of it,' advised her father when she went down to the kitchen where he was busy making tea for her mother to drink in bed. 'According to the radio it's going to break this evening and be changeable for two or three days. How did it go last night?'

'Fair,' said Thea. 'You should have been there.'

'Not when I'd a good book to read. There's a waiting list for it at the library.' The pause was brief. 'Your mother said Dave was there.'

'He showed his face.' Thea kept her own averted. 'He

was too concerned about leaving Mrs Barrington on her own to stay long.'

'Well, at least he made the effort.' Again the pause, longer this time. 'You and he getting along okay now?'

'We don't always see eye to eye,' she acknowledged with perfect truth. 'I think I might take Lady down to the cove later on. She'd probably appreciate a dip as much as I would.'

'Yes, well, be careful.' John Ralston lifted the set tray, tucking a magazine under his arm with an air of contentment. 'Best morning of the week. No surgery and no visits—unless I'm unlucky. Are you coming to church this morning?'

'I suppose I ought to,' she agreed. 'Although the thought of sitting through one of Mr Conniston's sermons is enough to put anyone off!'

Her father laughed. 'We all have to suffer for our sins.'

Including Dave? she wondered cynically, pouring herself a glass of orange juice. It was doubtful. But then he probably considered nothing of what he had said or done in any way wrong. It was for her own good, wasn't it? To give her a new slant on life. She was certainly getting that all right.

CHAPTER FIVE

As Thea had predicted, the service overran by a good twenty minutes, making it gone eleven when the congregation finally emerged into the bright sunshine. Going on ahead of her parents who lingered to chat with neighbours, she was changed and in the saddle before the half hour struck, cutting across the top of Springfield Wood to reach the cove.

Today the tide was far enough out to have exposed a route round to the adjoining bay which was inaccessible from the land. With a couple of hours to go before the turn, Thea felt safe enough in guiding Lady around the point.

There were caves in this part of the cliff. She and Gavin had explored them on a couple of occasions in the past. Today she didn't bother going beyond the entrance to the larger of the two, stripping down to the swimsuit she was already wearing beneath her jeans, and stashing the latter together with a towel across a rock where they would stay clear of sand.

With the mare's saddle draped over another rock, she had a little trouble in scrambling up on to the silky back, but she managed it in the end, gathering the reins in her hands and using her knees to urge the animal forward in the direction of the waves lapping the beach a couple of hundred feet away.

It was Mrs Templeton who had told her how much Lady loved the water, and that had proved something of an understatement. The mare revelled in it, wading out until the waves were lapping under her belly and standing there blissfully shaking her head at the spray whipped off the wave tops by the offshore breeze.

Thea left her to it, sliding from her back into the water and striking out for the far headland. The water felt good on her skin after that first small shock of immersion. A turn around the point, then she would head straight back again before Lady took it into her head to wander off in search of grass.

She had told Dave once that the currents around the island could be tricky, but this side was normally safe enough. Feeling the sudden pull on her legs, she knew a swift sense of panic, as swiftly squashed before it could take hold. She was going to need all her wits about her to get out of this, she thought, watching the headland move inexorably to her left as the current carried her right out past it. She had only just come under the influence, which suggested a fairly narrow channel running at an oblique angle out from the rocks, therefore if she turned about and swam hard at a cross angle she might escape from it before it carried her too far out.

Thinking about it was one thing, doing it quite another. By the time she did manage to break free of the deadly pull she was over a quarter of a mile from the shore and already nearing exhaustion from the sheer effort of the last few minutes. Away from the shelter of the land the wind was keen, the sea itself a great deal colder and rougher than she was accustomed to. Without a life-jacket to buoy her up, she found treading water almost as tiring as swimming, and floating was out of the question. If she was going to make it at all it would have to be on what slender reserves of strength she had left. Resolutely she turned her face towards the cliffs she could still see as the waves lifted her, and began to swim against the tide.

Before she had covered more than a few hundred

yards she knew she was going to fail. Her arms felt like
lead weights and she had ceased to make any headway
at all. She tried floating on her back again to rest her
limbs for a while, but even the effort required to keep
her head level in the water was more than she could
cope with. A wave broke over her face, and then another, bringing her chokingly upright. Panic flooded her,
robbing her of the last ounce of control. She threshed
frantically and immediately went under, taking in water
as she did so. She was going to die, she realised in
shock.

The hands reaching under her armpits were vice-like
in their grip, but she felt no pain, only a great surging
relief as sunlight hit her eyes again.

'Don't struggle!' Dave commanded as she made a
desperate attempt to turn in his grasp and grab on to
him. 'Hold still and I'll tow you in.'

Thea forced herself to do as he said, feeling the surge
as he went on to his back in the classic life-saving position and kicked out for the shore. She was safe now.
Dave wouldn't let her down. She was safe!

It took a long time to cover the distance. By the time
they could touch bottom Dave himself was almost
through. They staggered out of the water to collapse
together on the sand, lying supine with chests heaving
in unison. The blue sky above looked so tranquil, so
untouched. Hard to believe, Thea thought dazedly, that
anything nasty could happen on such a lovely day. If it
weren't for Dave she wouldn't be lying here now looking
at it. She would still be out there in the sea—beyond
looking at anything ever again.

A shudder ran through her, long and hard, drawing
her breath inwards on an audible sob. Dave spoke without moving.

'If you feel sick don't fight it. You must have swallowed quite a lot of water.'

'I'm all right.' Her voice sounded strangely disembodied, as if someone else was speaking for her from a great distance away. 'Thanks to you.' She paused, blinking back sudden, welling tears. 'How did you know? I mean, where——?'

'I came down for a swim,' he said, still without lifting his head. 'I saw Lady's hoofprints going round the end of the cove and followed them. You must have just swum into that current when I first saw you. You were moving pretty fast. Must be an underground river running into the bay along the point out there.'

'That's what it felt like. I've never swum this side before. There's only a few days in the year when the tide goes out far enough to get round.' She stopped again, swallowing thickly. 'Dave——'

'Don't dwell on it.' He pushed himself to his feet, holding out a hand to help her to hers. 'You need some warm dry clothes before reaction sets in. Where are they?'

'Over there,' waving a hand. 'By the cave.'

He put up his own hand and slicked back the dark hair from his forehead, eyes steady. 'Feeling strong enough to make it on your own, or do you want some help?'

She shook her head. 'I can manage, thanks.'

'In that case I'll go and gather my own things together.' His smile was dry. 'I can't remember the last time I got out of them so fast!'

Thea watched him move away down the beach towards the scattered garments obviously thrown off on the run. Clad only in dark blue trunks, his body was lean and hard, tapering from shoulder to hip without an ounce of surplus flesh in sight, and tanned deep brown. She swallowed again on some obstruction in her throat and turned to make for the cave.

Both horses were standing close up to the cliffs quietly doing nothing. Dave was riding the grey today, she noted. More highly bred than Major, the animal was normally inclined towards a certain nervousness in unfamiliar surroundings, but he seemed happy enough in Lady's company. Certainly neither had been in the least disturbed by the temporary disappearance of their human partners.

Towelled, and clad once more in jeans and shirt, Thea felt almost normal again. Almost but not quite. The shakiness which still invaded her limbs testifed to a lingering shock. She tried hard to conceal it as Dave came up the beach towards her, smiling a bright smile.

'Well, at least you got your swim, even if it was rather more strenuous than you probably intended. Can I interest you in a medal?'

There was no answering smile on the angular features. 'I don't want any medals,' he said. 'Just your promise that you won't swim alone again after this.'

'You mean here?' She laughed and shook her head. 'You can bet on it!'

'I mean anywhere.'

Thea stared at him, nonplussed. 'Oh, but that's ridiculous! I've been swimming in the cove round there since I was about eight, and more often than not alone.'

'So I'm overreacting.' He sounded totally unapologetic about it. 'I still want that promise.'

Thea bit her lip, aware that she owed him her life yet reluctant to commit herself to quite that extent. 'I'll willingly promise not to go into water I don't know on my own again,' she said at length. 'Will that do?'

He studied her for a moment before lifting his shoulders in a brief shrug. 'Seems it will have to.'

'Dave.' She put out an impulsive hand as he began to

turn away, already ashamed of her own ingratitude. 'I'm sorry, I'm just being pigheaded. Of course I'll promise.'

Just for a moment there was something in the grey eyes she couldn't fathom, then he relaxed again, his smile sudden and warming. 'No, you were right the first time. It would be ridiculous. You're a full-grown adult woman, not a kid.' His tone changed, taking a lighter note. 'On the other hand, if you do anything as stupid as this again I'll take it you've reverted and treat you accordingly. Right?'

'Right.' She was smiling with him, relieved to be back on even keel. 'I'll remember that.'

'You still look a bit shaken up,' he observed. 'Did you bring a flask?'

She nodded, indicating the two canvas bags down by Lady's saddle. 'Coffee, sandwiches, even oats for Lady. I intended staying down here for lunch.'

'We'll both stay,' he said. 'Unless you feel you'd be better off resting back home?'

'No.' The denial was swift. She met his eyes and shrugged wryly. 'I'd rather my mother didn't know about all this. It would only upset her.'

'With some cause.' He shook his head. 'I shan't tell her. As you say, there isn't much point. Let's get that coffee.'

The hot, aromatic liquid went a long way towards restoring normality—or as near to normality as things could get, Thea reflected, all too conscious of the man seated so close, his back against the same rock. The tang of the sea was on them both, stirring her senses in a way she found particularly disturbing. From now on whenever she smelled ozone up close it would remind her of Dave, she realised, and on an island this size that meant most of the time.

'Are you going to be staying on Sculla?' she heard

herself ask, and could have bitten off her tongue because it wasn't at all what she had meant to say.

He didn't turn his head. 'Do you want me to stay?'

She laughed, trying to sound suitably light about it. 'That's putting me into a cleft stick!'

This time he did look at her, an ironic look. 'You're not usually stuck for a straight answer.'

'I'm not usually as much in anyone's debt as I am in yours,' she countered. 'You saved my life a few minutes ago. That makes it doubly difficult to see straight.'

'Then forget about it,' he advised. 'Answer the way you would have done a couple of hours ago.'

'All right.' She paused, forcing herself to view matters objectively. 'I think you'd do Sculla a lot of good if you did stay. You already have. On the other hand, given the necessary authority, Gavin could and would do as much. You never knew your uncle. No amount of argument would get him to change his mind once he made it up. He set the figures each year for capital expenditure on the Estate, and once that was used there was no more forthcoming till the following year.'

'Then he wasn't fit to administer the trust,' Dave stated flatly. 'I've seen the original draft drawn up by Harry Barrington's legal advisers—or at least a copy of it. Any competent lawyer today could have found a way of forcing him to release sums adequate to requirements.'

'Only through the courts,' Thea protested. 'Gavin could hardly do that to his stepfather.'

'Not without making his own position a great deal less comfortable,' came the dry response. 'A matter of priorities, wouldn't you say?'

She was silent for a long moment digesting what had just been said. When she did speak it was on a more subdued note. 'Would you have done it?'

'If all else failed.'

'But you still don't believe all else should have failed.'

'No,' he said, 'I don't. Gavin can't even manage you.'

She stiffened. 'Even if that were true it's hardly the same thing.'

'It's true enough. Gavin's a follower, not a leader. Right now he's torn down the middle between you and his mother.'

Thea had come away from the rock, her back taut. 'That's as good as saying I manoeuvred him into asking me to marry him!'

'It wouldn't be the first time that has happened.' There was cynicism in his voice. 'You're not in love with him for sure.'

She was motionless, eyes fixed front. 'What makes you so certain?'

'This,' he said, and reached for her, pulling her down across him.

Her lips were stiff and unyielding at first, but not for long. Helplessly she found herself kissing him back, an arm curving about his neck to hold him closer. His chest was hard, crushing her breasts. Then the pressure was gone and his hand was there instead, the long, tensile fingers curving to the shape of her, exploring so slowly and sensuously she could scarcely contain the emotions growing in her.

'Is it like this with Gavin?' he murmured, lips at her ear. 'Does he rouse you this way?'

'No.' The admittance was torn from her. 'He doesn't have your—experience.'

His laugh came soft. 'If you were in love with him it wouldn't matter how inexpert he was at making love, you'd still prefer him to me. Why don't you take your head out of the sand, Thea? Gavin couldn't satisfy you.'

'That's not true!' She pulled away from him with a sudden sharp movement, fastening her shirt buttons with fingers that trembled. 'There's more to love than—*this*.'

'There might be,' Dave admitted, 'but without it you're going to find marriage desperately dull. That was the real Thea I was holding just now.'

'That was someone you conjured up because of what *you* are,' she flashed back. 'It didn't mean anything.'

He smiled faintly. 'It meant something to me. Maybe we should try conjuring her up again, and take it from there.'

'Don't touch me!' she snapped, then saw the derision in his eyes and subsided again wryly. 'All right, so I asked for that. You've every reason to think badly of me.'

'Not the same reason you're making out.' He paused, watching her, an odd expression in the grey eyes. 'Why don't you face up to it? It's a way of life you love, not a man. Married to Gavin you thought you could stay here on Sculla always. You didn't know about the line of inheritance until after Douglas died, did you? You imagined Gavin could simply take over where his stepfather left off.'

'No.' She was suddenly desperate to have him believe her. 'I never even thought about Douglas dying. Nobody did. He was the kind of man who could easily have gone on till he was a hundred.'

'So you weren't interested in becoming mistress of the manor,' Dave conceded. 'I can go along with that. You're not the avaricious type. All the same, you don't love Gavin. He's just a means to an end.'

'You're wrong.' Her voice sounded husky. 'I already told him I'd be willing to make a new life on the mainland.'

'Until it came to the point. Oh, sure, you'd go with him, but without Sculla there'd be nothing to hold you together. Janine sees it that way too.'

Green eyes flared. 'Did she put you up to this?'

It was a moment before he replied, and when he did it was with control. 'Nobody puts me up to anything. I'm just trying to make you see sense. You can't spend the rest of your life in a cocoon.'

'That's *my* decision.'

'Well, I'm making it mine.' Lean brown fingers fastened about her arm, holding her so she couldn't move away. There was ruthlessness in the line of his mouth. 'I'm not going to let it happen, Thea. You can count on that.'

She stared at him, jaw clenched. 'You can't stop it!'

'Can't I?' His grip tightened momentarily, then as suddenly relaxed, a smile curving his lips. 'Let's wait and see. Are you ready to go?'

Thea nodded, aware of mixed emotions. She had wanted Dave to make love to her again, she acknowledged numbly. Badly enough to undermine her better instincts. In his arms she was a different person. Staying out of them was the obvious answer. The question was, would he let her?

Gavin returned on the Wednesday by the inter-island boat bearing rough estimates from three of the firms he had contacted. The rest, he said, just hadn't wanted to know.

Dave picked him up from the harbour in the car and brought him back to the house as lunch was ready to be served, having called in at the Big Tree on the way. Seated at the table, Thea suspected that he had deliberately delayed their return in order to deny her a few minutes alone with her fiancé-to-be, although what difference that was going to make in the long run it was difficult to see. He could hardly keep them apart all the time.

If the last couple of days were anything to go by he might have lost interest in the whole affair, she reflected, listening with only half an ear to the two men talk. Certainly there had been no attempt to follow up Sunday's assault on her senses. Not that she would have wanted it, she hastened to assure herself. She couldn't afford to even think about it too much. What Dave could make her feel was purely physical, and not to be confused with any finer emotion. If Gavin couldn't elicit the same degree of arousal in her that was hardly his fault. She wouldn't want him to be that experienced, would she? One only had to imagine the number of women a man like Dave must have made love to in his time to get things into perspective.

'Is it going to take a long time, all this work?' asked Janine Barrington over dessert, growing bored with the conversation. 'If so I think I might take the opportunity to go and visit the Lesters in Gloucestershire. They've asked me often enough.'

'It might be a good time,' agreed Dave smoothly before anyone else could speak. 'The work isn't going to encroach on Whirlow too much, but there are one or two improvements I want making to the house while we're at it. The kitchens are antiquated. All credit to Mrs Murray for producing the meals she does in them, but it's more than time she had her job made easier.'

'That settles it,' Janine said decisively. 'Altering the kitchens will disrupt the whole household! When is it all likely to start?'

'Depends which firm we get to do the job. A couple of weeks if we accept Lawson's estimate.'

'It's the highest,' Gavin pointed out. 'They're a third up on Baileys.'

'But they've tackled this kind of contract work before, so they're likely to be more realistic about it,' countered his step-cousin. 'Both have excellent reputations, so there's nothing to be gained there. I'd say the main deciding factor is time. Baileys can't tackle the job before mid-August, and that means running on into harvest time.'

'How about the other?' suggested Gavin. 'They're appreciably lower, and they can start right away.'

Dave shook his head. 'They're too low.'

'It's only supposed to be a rough estimate.'

'Based on some pretty detailed figures. We sat up long enough preparing them. Then again, Lawson is the only one who mentions sending in an architect ahead of the team.'

'Lawson it is, then.' Gavin sounded resigned. 'I'll get on to it right away.'

'Fine.' Dave shifted his gaze. 'I saw your father in the village on my way down, Thea. He said they're ready to send young Paul Morrow home from hospital in the next couple of days.'

'Yes, he's apparently a whole lot better, although they're still not all that certain what was wrong with him.' She congratulated herself on the cool composure of her tone. 'I hope it stays calm for him. A rough crossing could set him right back.'

'What I was thinking too. I'm going over on the *Molly* in the morning to pick up the chopper I ordered. It's been flown down to Penzance for me. You know the boy—how do you think he's likely to react to a helicopter ride?'

'I'm not sure,' said Thea. 'I think it would depend who was with him.' She paused uncertainly. 'You're going to fly it yourself?'

'I'm qualified.' He sounded matter-of-fact about it.

'Later we'll do something about finding a regular pilot. The best way might be for you to come with me and fetch him out. We'd be home again by tea-time, all being well.'

'Dr Ralston would surely be the best person to go,' put in Gavin before Thea could form a reply. 'After all, the boy is his patient.'

'He does have others,' his cousin came back. 'He'd prefer not to spend another day away from the island.'

Thea said swiftly, 'You mean you've already discussed it with him?'

'That's right. As a matter of fact, he was the one who suggested you for the job. You're friendly with the family, I understand. The boy is likely to feel safer with someone he knows well.'

'I'm friendly with all the families on Sculla,' she responded a little tartly. 'I wouldn't have said Paul would feel any safer with me than anyone else he knows.'

'Except that you're the one who's being asked.'

Janine had an odd expression on her face. 'Perhaps Gavin could go with you instead,' she suggested.

'Gavin only just got back,' Dave said flatly. 'Anyway, I doubt if he'd be much comfort to a small boy.'

'You're right about that.' The younger man obviously didn't relish the thought at all. 'Looks as if it will have to be you, Thea. At least it will make a change for you.'

Green eyes met grey, the latter totally unreadable. Whatever Dave was thinking he was keeping it to himself. 'Well?' he asked.

'I don't seem to have any choice,' she said. 'The *Molly* leaves at eight sharp.'

'I know. I'll pick you up at seven forty-five. Gavin, you'll have to pick the car up from the harbour yourself if you want to use it tomorrow. I'll be flying straight in here to the house. Might be a good idea to have it standing by, then we can get young Paul home right away.'

'Where are you going to land?' asked Janine. 'Isn't there supposed to be some kind of marked out area?'

'Only where identification might be difficult. I can hardly miss Whirlow as a landmark, and the rear lawn is more than big enough.' He was glancing at his watch as he spoke. 'I want to give the mare a workout this afternoon, she's carrying too much weight.'

'My fault,' Janine admitted without particular concern. 'I don't ride as much these days. If it had been up to me I'd have got rid of all the horses when Douglas died. I never could see why he needed more than one mount for himself anyway.'

'He probably appreciated variety.' Dave got to his feet. 'I'll give coffee a miss. Gavin, you'll take care of that acceptance?'

'Of course.' The other man was affronted. 'I'm hardly likely to forget. Anything else you want seeing to this afternoon?'

'No. Have a rest.' Dave nodded briefly to them all and left.

'There goes a man who likes his own way,' remarked Janine to no one in particular. It was difficult to say whether she was admiring or criticising. Her glance rested fondly on her son. 'I'm glad you're back. David doesn't play chess the way you do.'

The answering smile was wry. 'You mean he wins. Were you serious about going to stay with the Lesters?'

'Yes, I was. I haven't seen anyone since Douglas died, and I can hardly ask people here if the whole place is going to be turned inside out.'

'It shouldn't be for too long,' Thea said placatingly. 'And it's going to be worth it in the end.'

'For whom?' the older woman demanded on a harder

note. 'You do realise Gavin's position here depends entirely on David's plans? If he stays he'll want to run the place himself, and I'm not going to stand by and see my son relegated to little more than an office clerk.'

'He won't stay.' Thea said it with a conviction that surprised even her, drawing a sharpened glance.

'He told you that?'

'Not in so many words,' she was bound to admit. 'I just know it, that's all.'

'Well, let's hope you're right, for all our sakes.' Putting down her coffee cup, Janine pushed back her chair. 'I'm going to go and phone the Lesters while I'm still in the mood. Tell Linda I'll have tea upstairs, will you, Thea. I've some letters to write.'

Gavin poked contemplatively at the sugar with a spoon as his mother left the room. Only when the door had closed behind her did he speak.

'What makes you so sure about Dave's future plans if he hasn't discussed them with you?'

'It's as I said,' she responded, striving for the right note. 'An instinct. He doesn't have an island mentality. He's used to the wide open spaces. A few weeks on Sculla and he'll be more than ready to leave.'

He was looking at her now with the same thoughtful consideration he had applied to the sugar. 'You got to know him pretty well in a few days.'

'I don't know him at all,' she denied. 'I doubt if anyone ever got close enough. Why don't you ask him yourself?'

'I did, and he told me he'd let me know what he'd decided when he'd had time to do any deciding. You seem surer of him than he does of himself.'

'There's always a chance that I'm wrong.' She stirred restlessly. 'Did you want to give me that letter right away? You must have had an early start this morning.'

'Yes, I did.' He sounded suddenly rueful. 'Sorry about the inquisition. I've missed you these last few days.'

'Me too.' She said it warmly, eager to convince them both. 'You know, you haven't even said hallo properly yet.'

'That's easily remedied.' He got up and came to where she sat, bending to press a kiss to her lips. 'Will that do?'

'For now.' She kept the smile fixed. 'Are you sure you don't mind me going off tomorrow?'

'Well, it's a bit short notice considering I've been away almost a week, but I daresay I can cope for one day.'

It wasn't what she had meant, but she let it lie. Telling him the truth wouldn't help. She had to work this whole thing out for herself.

CHAPTER SIX

THE crossing in the *Molly* was one of the most comfortable Thea had ever experienced, the sea almost flat calm. They made good time, putting into harbour a good fifteen minutes ahead of schedule.

'I'm not due to make the pick up until two,' said Dave when they disembarked, 'but I might wander along to the heliport and make sure everything is okay. For what they're charging to use the pad it certainly should be!' He stood on the quay side, hands thrust into the pockets of his light-coloured slacks. 'How about you? Do you have any shopping you want to do?'

Thea nodded, avoiding his eyes. 'It's market day. I promised Mom I'd look out for some curtain material if I got the chance.'

'So we'll meet up for lunch. Where do you suggest?'

'There's a little place in Chapel Street,' she said. 'The Chef's Hat, it's called. It's nothing fancy, but the food is good.'

'All right, I'll see you there at twelve-thirty. We can fetch young Paul from the hospital by taxi after we've eaten.' The pause was brief. 'Don't get lost.'

She watched him walk away from her, seeing other female heads among the holiday crowds turn to look after him too. There had been no sign on the way over that this trip was anything but what it was purported to be. In all fairness it could hardly be anything else. Her father had confirmed that much last night.

He would have gone himself, he had said, but he was concerned about one of his young married patients due to have her first baby any time. Thea was only too well aware of the possibility of complications where there was no previous history to provide guide lines. Only last year they had almost lost Laura Crossley when she went into premature labour. The helicopter was going to be of tremendous value in getting first-timers across to the mainland hospital should the need arise.

The town was packed, the market place a seething mass of humanity. Thea found a stall selling materials, and managed to secure six yards of an attractive green and white print which would brighten up the pine kitchen back home far better than the present faded gingham. Some dark green mugs on another stall nearby caught her eye. She bought four as a present, knowing her mother would like them. The limited range of goods available for purchase on Sculla was one drawback nobody could deny.

By twelve-fifteen she had completed her shopping list, as far as it went, having bought as much as she could comfortably carry. Dave was already waiting outside the café when she got there.

'We might not be able to leave as planned,' he said when they were seated at a table near the door. 'There's a sea fog come in during the last hour. They've already suspended all service flights.'

Thea looked at him in concern, weighing the implications. 'What about Paul? We're supposed to pick him up after lunch.'

'I phoned the hospital and explained the situation. They'll hold him until we can get away.' The mockery was faint but discernible. 'Don't worry, it could lift any time.'

Thea doubted it. The last time this had happened the *Molly* had not returned to Sculla for forty-eight hours and conditions had been very similar to what they were today. Unless a stiff breeze got up they could finish up being stuck here overnight.

'We could walk down and have a word with Cap'n George if it hasn't lifted by the time we've finished lunch,' she suggested. 'He might have some idea of how long it's likely to last.'

'Why not?' The agreement was easy enough, but there was a definite glint in the grey eyes. 'It will give us something to do. Does everybody always give him his title the way you do?'

'Well, yes.' Thea had to smile. 'He used to have this inseparable drinking partner with the same name. He was Farmer George. Island people only use surnames as a last resort—among themselves, at any rate. I'd be surprised if many even remember the Vicar's. His wife is either Maureen or Mrs Vicar, depending on the age group.'

'It's a close community,' Dave agreed. 'And an unusual one. No policeman, for instance. I always thought the village constable was mandatory in England.'

'We don't have any crime,' she came back. 'Oh, you get the young ones up to the usual mischief, but they're none of them allowed to run wild. If they're caught raiding orchards or anything like that, they get a clip round the ear and a promise to tell their parents if it happens again. It doesn't often. Dad always says the swift sharp shock carries more weight than any amount of reasoned discussion.'

'I'm sure he's right.' Dave sounded thoughtful. 'You know, I can imagine a lot of people might like to spend a little time lapping up the atmosphere on a place like Sculla. No crime, no crowds, no busy roads to contend with—a real get-away-from-it-all vacation.'

Thea looked at him sharply. 'What are you thinking?'

'Just what a marvellous country-style hotel Whirlow

would make. Limit the numbers, of course. Say no more than a dozen guests at any one period. That alone would be enough to have people fighting to get here.'

'We've never had holidaymakers on Sculla,' she said. 'Apart from the odd camper or two.' She paused uncertainly. 'You're not serious?'

'I could be. The house needs something doing with it.'

'What about Mrs Barrington? You promised her a home at Whirlow for as long as she wanted it.'

'She'd still have it. One wing could remain private. On the other hand, she'd have company when she felt like it—in season, at least. The kind of people who'd be attracted to a place like Sculla wouldn't be rowdies looking for fun and games. They'd be peace-lovers. It would create a few extra jobs on the island too.'

In spite of herself, Thea was beginning to see the possibilities in the idea. Whirlow had stood half empty for too long. It would be good to see it come to life again, even if only for a part of the year.

'It would take some getting used to,' she said with caution.

'It would take some preparing for,' Dave returned equably. 'There are six bedrooms in the west wing, and they all need bringing up to scratch. Next season would be the one to aim for.'

They continued to toss the subject around throughout the meal, adding detail as they went. Almost all foodstuffs could be home-grown or reared, which meant fresh every day. Good plain English cooking should be the order of the day, with no fancy sauces to smother the taste of the meat. To get around the island visitors could have the choice of horse or bicycle, dependent on taste and inclination.

'You could open up the billiards room again for the

evenings,' Thea suggested over coffee, warming to the theme by the minute. 'And there's at least a couple of card tables tucked away somewhere. Do you think they might be bored without television?'

Dave shook his head. 'That could be one of the biggest attractions. It's the biggest killer of conversation I know.'

'Yes.' Her tone was reminiscent. 'The relations I stayed with in Exeter used to have it on almost constantly in the evenings, even though they were always grumbling about the quality of the programmes. There are one or two who'd like to receive it on Sculla, but the majority aren't interested. We have radio, and that's good enough.' She paused there, conscious of having strayed from the point. 'I'm sorry, that's by the way. I think it might work, Dave. It might take a little time for people to accept it, but they'd get used to the idea.'

He smiled. 'The way you have?'

'Oh, hardly as quickly,' she laughed. 'I'm more adaptable than most.'

'That's good.' His tone was light. 'The more so the better. Did you want some more coffee?'

'No, thanks.' She pushed away the cup and saucer in unnecessary emphasis, mood changing abruptly. 'I suppose we should go and check on the weather. We might be lucky.'

Luck, however, was out. The mist had moved in over the harbour itself, shrouding everything in the same shifting greyness. The *Molly* was still tied up at her berth, the dock deserted. They found George Yelland sitting with his feet up in the wheelhouse reading a newspaper.

'Doubtful if anybody's going to get out today,' he stated comfortably in answer to Thea's query. 'This little lot isn't going to lift without some wind, and that isn't due to pick up before tonight.'

'You won't be attempting to get back tonight your-self, then?' asked Thea, knowing full well what the answer would be.

It came pat. 'Only a fool would try for Sculla in this. Since when did you take to asking stupid questions, girl?'

'I was thinking about Mom and Dad,' she defended hastily. 'I suppose I can always phone through and let them know the situation.'

'If they don't already. It must have been on the one o'clock weather.'

'Of course.' She avoided looking at Dave. 'Well, I'll phone them anyway.'

'Do it from the hotel,' Dave suggested. 'We're going to have to find rooms for the night.'

'Might not be so easy this time of year,' observed Cap'n George. 'Place gets full up with tourists.' The last on a disparaging note. 'If you have any trouble you could try out an old friend of mine—widow woman name of Harley.' The faded blue eyes challenged them to make any comment. 'She lets out rooms from time to time when she feels like it. I'll jot down the address.'

Dave took the scrap of paper from him. 'Thanks. That might come in useful. Thea, we may as well make a start.'

'There's still a chance it might lift in time,' she insisted, not moving. 'Surely we can leave booking a hotel until later on when we're sure.'

'Not unless you want to finish up begging a bed at the hospital alongside young Paul.' He sounded faintly impatient. 'We can't go dragging him out at a moment's notice either. It would mean them keeping him at the ready for the rest of the day.'

'It won't shift before the tide turns,' said George with

authority. 'And not even then without wind. I'd say we're all going to have to spend the night here.'

Thea gave in; there was little else she could do under the circumstances. 'All right,' she said with reluctance.

'Cheer up,' Dave chided on the familiar mocking note when they were on dry land again. 'It won't be so bad. If you're good I might even take you out to dinner.'

'I'm not dressed for going out,' was all she could find to say.

His glance took in her jeans and silky white shirt without change of expression. 'You look fine to me. I'm not exactly formal myself.'

'I don't even have a toothbrush,' she murmured.

'So we buy the essentials.' This time the impatience was marked. 'Accept it, will you? We're not going to get back to Sculla tonight, and we're going to have to make the best of it. Just for once in your life forget about that damned island!'

It wasn't Sculla she was thinking about right now, but she was hardly going to admit it. Better he should think that than be made aware of the truth. Being with Dave at all was a danger to her equilibrium, spending a whole evening in his company was going to tax her resources to the full. For Gavin's sake as well as her own, she had to make the effort to stay aloof.

Finding accommodation for the night proved as difficult as George had predicted. It was Dave who finally made the decision to go straight to Mrs Harley rather than waste any more time and effort.

The address the Captain of the *Molly* had given them lay towards the top of the town on a narrow street made even narrower by parked cars along its length. The house itself was three-storeyed and at least a hundred years old, standing back behind a minuscule front garden and badly in need of a lick of paint.

Not exactly prepossessing, Dave commented, but beggars couldn't be choosers. He led the way firmly to the front door.

Mrs Harley answered the bell herself. She was a woman in her mid-sixties, unashamedly stout and of a plain but cheerful countenance.

'If George Yelland sent you, of course I've got room,' she said. 'My old man and him were real good pals. Double, is it?'

'Two singles,' Thea put in before Dave could answer. 'We're not married.'

'I didn't think it made all that much difference these days,' returned their hostess without blinking an eye. 'Just the one night, did you say?'

'I hope so.' This time it was Dave who did the answering. 'If the mist lifts we'll be away in the morning.'

'Travelling by car, are you?' asked Mrs Harley, leading the way up a broad oak-railed staircase. 'Lots of folk driving round the West Country this time of year.'

'We're from Sculla,' said Thea. 'We came over with Cap'n George this morning before the fret came in.'

'From Sculla, eh? Should have known when you said the name. George told me there was a new owner.'

'Not really owner,' Dave corrected. 'Trustee. There's a difference.'

'Not to my way of thinking.' She paused at the head of the staircase, a hand pressed to her side. 'Just catch my breath a minute. Got to lose some weight, the doc says, but I don't know how. Only real pleasure I get is eating.' She started off again, heavy in her movements. 'It's just along here. Two rooms with the bath between—best I can do.'

Like the hall and staircase, the rooms were spotless. One of them had a double bed covered in a white lace spread which looked old enough to be valuable.

'I'll take this one,' offered Thea from the doorway of the smaller room farther along the landing. Her laugh was over-bright. 'It seems strange not having any luggage to unpack.'

'I'd offer you the use of a clean nightie if I had one that wouldn't fit you four times over,' chuckled Mrs Harley. 'Still, my daughter always used to say there's nothing healthier than sleeping in the nude. She might be right at that. Never had a cold in her life, that girl, until she got married and started wearing all these fancy see-through things. Waste of time, I call it. What man wouldn't rather touch nice warm skin than keep catching his fingernails in all that nylon!'

Thea didn't dare look at Dave, who had appeared behind the widow in time to hear at least the latter observation. Mrs Harley was a character and a half by any standards. Cap'n George might very well have had his tongue tucked into his cheek in sending them here in the first place.

'Well, I'll leave you to it, then,' said the woman. 'The door's always open if you want to go out. These doors don't have locks, but you don't have anything to steal, do you?' She didn't bother to wait for any answer to that one, turning to pass Dave in the doorway. 'By the way,' she added over a shoulder, 'I don't do any cooking except breakfast.'

'That's all right,' said Dave. 'We'll be going out for dinner. Will seven-thirty be okay for breakfast?'

'Suits me. I'm always up at six.'

There was silence for a moment or two after she had gone. Thea walked to the long, narrow window and looked out over rooftops down towards where the sea would be on a better day. Right now there was nothing to be seen but the same opaque greyness, with fingers here and there creeping into the town.

'It's only just gone four,' she said without turning her head. 'What do we do for the next few hours until dinner time?'

The moment she had spoken she wished she could retract the question. She could sense Dave's sardonic lift of the mobile left eyebrow even through the back of her head.

'We need to do some shopping,' he reminded her. 'And you wanted to phone your mother, didn't you? There's a telephone in the hall. I'm sure Mrs Harley will let you use it. I'll wait up here till you're finished.'

She had to turn round then, meeting the grey eyes with what equanimity she could muster. 'I only need a toothbrush and some paste. Perhaps you could buy for us both.' The pause held deliberation. 'You can always stop the cost out of my salary.'

The glint was sudden and dangerous. 'Or in kind. Any particular brand?'

Thea shook her head, already regretting the implied challenge. Dave was not a man to play word games with—or any other kind, for that matter. 'It isn't important.'

'Right, then I'll see you in half an hour or so.'

He was gone before she could say anything, moving off along the landing and down the stairs with firm tread. Thea waited until the outer door had closed behind him before she stirred herself to follow his footsteps.

She found Mrs Harley in the kitchen feeding three cats of varying colouring and indeterminate breeding.

'Help yourself,' she invited in answer to Thea's request. 'You'll have to go through the operator for Sculla.'

'Yes, I know,' Thea acknowledged. 'I can't imagine

the G.P.O. ever getting around to putting Sculla on
S.T.D. Anyway, it would spoil our switchboard operator's whole life if she didn't have any calls to listen in
to!'

It took several minutes to make the connection. Her
mother answered.

'It's me,' said Thea. 'I'm afraid we're not going to
make it back tonight. It's thick mist right along the
coast.'

'So it said on the local weather report. It isn't too
good here either.' The voice was faint, distorted by
interference on the line. 'Where are you?'

'Staying with a friend of Cap'n George—a Mrs
Harley. Paul's still at the hospital.'

'Oh.' The pause seemed to last a long time. 'Well,
that's all right, then. Are you going to ring Gavin?'

'Could you do it for me?' Thea asked on impulse.
'The lines are bad—I can barely hear you. Tell him we'll
be home in the morning, all being well. Dave says flying
time shouldn't be much more than twenty minutes once
we get up.'

'All right.' The voice faded, then came on again, '. . .
care.'

'We will,' Thea assured her, taking a calculated
gamble on what she had missed. ' 'Bye, Mom. See you
tomorrow.'

'Get through all right?' asked Mrs Harley from
the kitchen doorway. That the question was purely
rhetorical was demonstrated when she added, 'Flying
back, did you say? I didn't know the service went to
Sculla.'

'It doesn't,' Thea confirmed. 'This one is privately
owned by the Estate.'

'Nice.' The woman looked suitably impressed. 'Make
things a lot easier.' She paused as a thought obviously

struck her. 'What about George, though? Will the *Molly* be needed now?'

Thea smiled. 'As much as ever. The helicopter is for use in emergencies and where weather conditions make it difficult for the *Molly* to make the crossing. It can't carry the load Cap'n George brings across every morning and night. Dave—Mr Barrington realises that.'

'Is he going to stay on Sculla, then?' Mrs Harley sounded surprised. 'I wouldn't have thought a man like him would stand being cooped up on a little island.'

So even a complete stranger recognised that fact, thought Thea, trying to feel glad of it. With Dave gone all, or at least most, of Gavin's problems would be solved. Still, it was hardly going to be immediate, was it? He would surely want to stay and see the repairs and renovations he had instigated put into effect.

She was in her room when he returned. The tap on her door brought her to her feet from her seat on the bed to cross the narrow space and open it.

'One toothbrush,' he said, handing her a brown paper bag, 'plus one tube of paste. And this,' giving her a larger plastic carrier with the name of a store on the front, 'might make you feel a little less vulnerable tonight. I had to make a guess at the size.' He smiled jeeringly at the expression on her face. 'Just a gift, no strings attached. See you around seven.'

His own door had opened and closed again behind him before she moved to do likewise with hers. The carrier contained a pair of plain blue cotton pyjamas of a style which should have gone out with the Ark. Gazing at them, Thea wondered furiously if he really imagined she wore such garments in bed or was simply having a joke at her expense. Neither explanation appealed.

I hate him, she told herself, and wished it were only as simple as that. What she felt about Dave came under no category she had ever plumbed in depth before. She was more than a little afraid to start doing it now.

Apart from taking a shower there was little to do towards preparing for the evening. She had brought along a lipstick and that was all in the way of make-up.

She heard the water start running again as she put a comb through her hair, and reckoned Dave would be at least another fifteen minutes. For a wild moment or two she actually contemplated developing a headache and crying off the whole evening, but she doubted if he was going to believe her. She was making too much of the whole thing anyway, she reassured herself. Whatever plans Dave might have, it was up to her just how far she followed them.

She had been wrong about how long it would take him to shower and dress. He was ready and knocking on her door within ten minutes, dark hair still damp, jaw freshly shaved. All doors were closed when they went downstairs, Mrs Harley not in evidence. A white Escort stood on the road outside the iron gateway.

'Best I could do at short notice,' said Dave, opening the near door for her. 'At least it will get us where we want to go. The man at the hire company gave me the name of a place out on the Hayle Road, so I rang through and booked a table for eight.'

'I thought you were gone rather a long time,' Thea commented. She waited a brief moment before adding without expression, 'Thanks for the pyjamas.'

He slid behind the wheel, his smile ironical. 'Real passion-killers, aren't they? Wearing those you don't need a lock on the door.'

She glanced at him sharply, began to speak and abruptly changed her mind. He was no fool; he knew what she had been thinking, and this was his way of telling her she had nothing to fear from him. What she had to guard against was the deep down part of her that almost wished she did.

Their destination proved to be a small and unpretentious hotel set back from the road on a corner. Inside it was all olde-worlde charm—a great deal of it genuine. Horse-brasses festooned the huge stone fireplace in the bar, while another wall bore prints of old Cornwall, many of them dealing with the tin mines which had formed such a great part of the Cornish economy in the not so distant past.

'We decide what we want to eat through here,' Dave announced, returning from the bar itself with their drinks and copy of the menu. 'They're a bit short on these, so we'll have to share. What do you fancy?'

'Nothing substantial,' Thea returned, running an eye down the typed page. 'I had a big lunch.'

'You hardly need to worry about your figure.' His tone was light. 'In fact an extra pound or two wouldn't go amiss. How about the mixed grill?'

'I don't mind.' The comment had stung a little; she was trying hard not to let it show. 'We can always ask for a doggie bag for what I can't manage to eat. Mrs Harley's breakfasts might not be as substantial as Mrs Murray's.'

He gave her a fleeting glance. 'You've spent nights at Whirlow?'

'Only one,' she admitted. 'Mom and Dad went over to visit my aunt on St Mary's, and got held over by a storm. Gavin didn't like the idea of me spending the night alone in the house.'

'Even on Sculla. What could have harmed you?'

'Not a lot, but he didn't see it that way. His mother was there too.'

The laugh came low. 'I doubt if it would have made much difference. Gavin doesn't strike me as the type to go breaking down the kind of barriers you put up.'

Her chin lifted. 'What makes you so sure I put up any barriers where Gavin's concerned?'

'Intuition, plus a little basic psychology. You want a ring on your finger before you let any man into your bed. Right?'

Thea said stiffly, 'I was brought up to believe that was the right way.'

'Except where it turns out to be the wrong man. Marriages have foundered on sexual incompatibility.'

Not his, came the thought. If and when Dave Barrington married it would be to a woman who matched his blueprint in every respect. Thea could even picture her: a tall, blonde Swedish type, all cool and composed on the surface and hot melting passion within.

'We've been through all this before,' she pointed out. 'I'd prefer to leave it.'

'And I'd prefer not.' His jaw had a stubborn jut. 'I'm out to make you admit it.'

'Admit what?'

'That sex is important to you.'

'I never said it wasn't.' She kept her tone level. 'I just don't happen to think it's *all*-important.'

'Only because you've never experienced it in any finite sense.'

'The waitress is coming over,' Thea muttered between her teeth. 'Will you please shut up!'

Dave did so with a dry little smile, half turning in his seat to speak to the girl as she came to a halt with pad and pencil poised. Thea took advantage of the moment to slide from her seat, moving towards the rear of the room with all the confidence of one who knew exactly where she was going.

Safe in the ladies' powder room, she sat down in front of the solitary mirror and took an assessing look at the image reflected there. Not bad, but not brilliant either, she concluded. Certainly not a face to launch a thousand ships—or even one, for that matter. If only Dave would leave her alone and stop trying to make her into something she wasn't! All he had succeeded in doing was making her restless, uncertain of what she really wanted any more. Comparing Gavin with Dave made the former seem dull, yet it was hardly a fair assessment. Dave hadn't spent the greater part of his life on a small island.

He greeted her return with questioning concern. 'You took off in rather a hurry. Are you feeling okay?'

'Perfectly, thanks. You know, you've hardly ever mentioned your part of the world since you've been here,' she added, determined to give him no further opportunity to get at her. 'Just whereabouts in Natal is your farm?'

'About fifty miles north-west of Durban. Nearest town is Colesburg, population about eight thousand.'

'What do you grow?'

'Fruit mostly—pineapple and banana. Sugar is the main crop in the area. My land adjoins one of the few privately owned plantations left, Breckonsridge it's called.' He paused briefly. 'Brad married an English girl a few years back. She wasn't unlike you when she first came out. There was no place like home.'

'And now?' Thea asked, drawn despite herself.

He laughed. 'Breckonsridge *is* her home. They've got a couple of kids and do a lot of entertaining, so she's pretty well occupied. Her braiis are legend.'

'That's a kind of barbecue, isn't it?'

'The original. We eat out of doors whenever possible back home. Even in winter it's rarely too cold.'

'It sounds lovely,' she acknowledged. 'You must find England very different.'

'England, yes, Sculla, no—apart from the weather.'
He rolled his glass between his hands, watching the
movement of the liquid within. 'You should come and
see it some day.'

He had said 'come', she noted with a pang, not 'go'.
So he really did intend to go back to South Africa.
Suspecting was one thing, having it confirmed quite
another. She felt suddenly depressed.

If he noted any change in her mood during the rest of
the evening he made no comment. The food was excellent, the wine he chose rich and fruity without being too
heavy. For once Thea made no effort to stop her glass
being refilled. She needed the lift it was giving her.

'I've been down to have a look at the *Sea Queen*,' Dave
said at one point. 'She'll need some work doing on her
before she goes into deep water again—there's a hole
right through the port bow.'

'That must have happened the day your uncle had his
heart attack,' Thea reasoned. 'He'd gone out with
Gavin—just the two of them. Gavin had to bring her in
alone.' She caught the faint change of expression in the
grey eyes and flushed a little. 'He isn't very good with
boats. He only used to go at all to please his stepfather.'

'He doesn't seem very good at any of the things you
like doing,' Dave remarked. 'What *are* his interests?'

'Music,' she said. 'Reading. His work.' She tried to
think of something more riveting to add and couldn't,
tagging on defensively, 'All of which I share.'

'Perhaps as well, considering,' was all the answer she
got.

Dave showed little inclination to chat during the drive
back to Penzance. He seemed preoccupied with his own
thoughts. Thea was the same, except that in her case she
dared not allow herself to dwell too deeply. Nothing
was straightforward any more, she knew that much. She

wasn't sure how she felt about anything—or anyone.

Only when they breasted the last rise did she come to life, sitting up straighter in her seat to gaze in wonderment at the clear moonlit seascape.

'The mist is gone!' she exclaimed unnecessarily. 'I wonder what time that happened?'

'Too late to be of any use,' Dave responded. 'At least we're assured of an early start in the morning. If Mrs Harley is still up we'll ask for breakfast at seven instead of half past. We can pick Paul up from the hospital and be in the air by eight. All right by you?'

'As early as you like,' she agreed. 'The sooner we're home the better.'

'Back where it's safe—where you're not likely to be tempted?' His tone was light enough on the surface but with an underlying edge. 'I realise tonight hasn't been a very memorable occasion, but it isn't over yet. Are you likely to scream if I come to your room later on?'

'It's doubtful,' she said, attempting to match his mood. 'I'd appeal to your better nature.'

'And if I proved not to have one?'

'Then I might scream.'

'Pity.' There was no humour in the line of his mouth. 'I must remember to bring along a gag.'

'Dave, stop it,' she said on an unsteady note. 'You're not being funny.'

'I never intended to be.' His glance was fleeting, but long enough to reveal purpose in the grey eyes. 'It's more than time you learned what it's all about.'

'More comparisons?' she got out, refusing to take the threat seriously. 'The professional versus the amateur. I can tell you now which I'd prefer.'

'You can tell me anything you like,' he came back. 'Proving it is something else.'

Thea stayed silent, recognising the futility in trying to

top him on a verbal exchange. He wouldn't do anything.
He was just trying to shake her up. And succeeding, she
had to admit.

The house was in darkness when they reached it, but
the door, as promised, was unlocked. Dave bolted it
securely the moment they were safely inside, then flicked
a switch to light their way upstairs, motioning Thea
ahead of him. She climbed a trifle unsteadily, lightheaded from too much wine and too vitally aware of
the man at her back. Only when he failed to stop at his
own doorway did she pause and turn, blocking the
narrow landing.

'Goodnight,' she said with emphasis.

He made no answer, just pulled her to him, his mouth
finding hers in a kiss that banished resistance far more
effectively than any words could have done, crystallising
her emotions into one urgent desire. She made only a
token protest when he lifted her in her arms, suddenly
not caring any more—not even caring if Mrs Harley
heard them.

There was a fleeting return to sanity when he laid her
down on the bed in her room, but that faded the
moment he started kissing her again. She had never felt
this way with Gavin, never known this kind of longing.
It didn't matter how many other women Dave had made
love to in his time providing he kept right on doing it to
her.

He took off her shirt with practised ease, and as
adroitly removed his own, bringing her back to him with
a faint sigh of satisfaction. 'That's better,' he murmured
against her lips. 'Now I can feel you. Is that good,
Thea?'

'Yes.' Her eyes were closed, her back arched in-
stinctively to bring them even closer together. 'Oh, yes!'

'And this?' He slid a hand between them, circling one

breast with a sensitivity that sent tremor after tremor racing through her body. His mouth moved lower, scoring a long slow passage down the length of her throat and into the valley between her breasts before finally finding its mark. The touch of his tongue on her flesh was agony, drawing in her breath on a sharp, gasping sound. She slid her hands into the thickness of his hair, holding him closer, murmuring words deep in her throat without even being aware of what she was saying.

'Enough?' he asked softly. 'Do you want me to stop?'

She didn't have to think about the answer, was incapable of thinking about anything rationally. 'No,' she breathed.

'Well, I'm going to have to,' he said, 'while I still can.' He sat up with a convulsive movement, a wry little smile on his lips. 'It's the wine doing most of the thinking for you. You had over half the bottle.'

She lay gazing up at him with stunned eyes, shocked back to sobriety. He had just been playing with her, she realised. He hadn't really wanted to make love to her. It had all been a game!

'Don't look at me as if I were some kind of monster,' he said. 'I'm trying my damnedest not to be. I took a mean advantage just now.'

'I'm not drunk.' Her throat hurt so much she could scarcely get the words out.

'Not to notice,' he agreed. 'But enough to affect your reactions. If I took you now it would be because you'd lost the ability to say no, not because you wanted me enough to ignore any other inclinations. If and when we make love I want you in full possession of all your faculties—able to make your own decisions without having them forced on you.'

She became suddenly conscious of her semi-nudity

and had to forcibly restrain herself from bringing her
arms across her breasts. It was a little late for that kind
of modesty now. 'Go away,' she said thickly. 'Just go
away, and leave me alone!'

'Not while you're feeling the way you do.' Dave got
up and moved to the window, looking out into the
darkness with hands thrust deep into pockets. 'I want
you, Thea, but I'm not having you this way.'

'You're not having me at all!' She sat up, reaching for
her shirt with groping fingers and pulling it around her.
'I suppose I should be grateful for your compunction!'

'I don't give a damn whether you're grateful or not.'
His tone was curt. 'I'm telling you what I feel. It takes a
certain type of man to use a woman just because she's
there and available. Next time I'll rouse you without the
drink to help it along.'

'I told you, there won't be a next time.' She had her
back turned to him, rigid as a board, her fingers clutch-
ing the front of her shirt. 'Please go, Dave.'

It seemed a long time before he moved, picking up
his own shirt from the bed in passing. 'Maybe I should
have carried right on,' he said cynically. 'My better
nature doesn't seem to have stood me in very good
stead.'

The urge to call him back was like a shout inside her,
but she resisted it. He might have been speaking the
truth when he said he wanted her, but that was all he
felt. Gavin loved her, and she loved him. That was more
important than any of this.

CHAPTER SEVEN

PAUL was ready and waiting at eight when they got there. 'He's been on tenterhooks since he woke at five,' the Ward Sister told Thea, handing over the tiny suitcase. 'I should think the whole hospital must know he's going home in a helicopter! He's talked about little else since he heard about it.'

'And we were afraid he might be nervous!' Thea laughed, taking hold of the small, thin hand. 'Your mum can't wait to see you again, Paul.'

Dark eyes beamed up at her happily. 'I hope she's got some ice-cream. I've had ice-cream every day here!'

'He needs building up again,' said the Sister with an indulgent look. It was easy to see that the child had been a favourite with the staff. 'There's a balanced diet sheet in his file for Dr Ralston. You will make sure he gets it, won't you?'

'He's my father,' Thea acknowledged. 'I'll pass it on to him myself. Ready, Paul?'

Dave had been standing back at the ward doors waiting, and he grinned easily at the boy as the trio approached. 'Hi, feller!'

'Are you the pilot?' demanded Paul.

'That's right.' Dave put out a hand and took the suitcase from Thea. 'Let's go.'

The journey down to the heliport took only minutes. They left the car in the parking lot from where it was to be picked up by the hire company. Finished in shining white with a single green stripe, the machine in which they were to fly was all ready for them. A four-seater, it could have held all three of them in front without much difficulty, but Thea chose to go in the back, after seeing Paul strapped securely into his seat beside the pilot at his own request.

She had never flown in a helicopter before, and found the noise shattering at close quarters. They lifted to a couple of hundred feet before moving off to the south-west on a route which would take them right out over the tip of Cornwall at Gwennap Head.

Flying at such a height it was easy to pick out land-marks. The coastline itself was a mass of coves, some rocky, some with sandy beaches pale enough to look almost white in the morning sunlight. Paul was in ecstasy, nose pressed against the glass at his side, the comments coming thick and fast. Dave answered all his questions with easy tolerance, bringing them down lower still when they left the land behind to give the child a close-up of the white curling wave tops as they sped along.

Thea watched it all with only partial attention, her thoughts turned inwards. There had been little in Dave's attitude this morning to suggest that he even re-membered last night, yet he could hardly have forgotten. Perhaps his was the best way: pretend it never happened. Only that wasn't going to be so easy, not with her senses still tuned to him the way they were. Even now she wanted desperately to be close to him, to feel his hands holding her, the lean hardness of his body. She would get over it because she had to get over it—because there was no future in yearning for a man who had his own life to live and intended to do it—but it was going to take time.

They came in low over Sculla, causing heads to lift and fingers to point. Paul waved right back, calling out names as he recognised various people.

'Can we fly over my house?' he begged. 'Can we?'

Dave smiled and nodded. 'You'll have to show me where it is.'

'Over there.' A small finger jabbed excitedly at the glass. 'See that lane? My house is right at the end of it.'

Finding it, Dave circled it twice, bringing Nora Morrow to the door, a hand going up to her mouth as she looked up at the bright machine. Paul waved until his arm almost fell off, shouting out that he would be home soon in total disregard of the fact that she couldn't possibly have heard him.

Whirlow came into view bare moments later, the rear lawn a broad green expanse well clear of the trees bordering the grounds. Once again figures appeared from various directions, stopping at a safe distance to watch the helicopter put down.

They landed with scarcely a bump and Dave immediately cut the engine. The cessation of sound was like being struck deaf for a moment before the ears adjusted to normal. He was out before the rotors had stopped spinning, telling them both to stay where they were until he came round to let them out.

He took Thea first, helping her down with hands about her waist. For an emotive few seconds the firm mouth was only inches from hers, his breath warm on her cheek. She avoided his eyes by looking over his shoulder to where she could see Gavin standing on the terrace, thankful when her feet found solid earth.

Paul skipped clear the moment he was on the ground, running wild in sheer exhilaration. Thea caught him before he could overtire himself, aware that his thin little body was not yet ready for too much exertion. She was still holding on to him when they reached the terrace, her smile strained as Gavin came to meet them.

'That was quite a trip,' he said. 'Thank heaven the weather improved.'

'It could have been worse,' she agreed. 'Do you have the car here, Gavin? I'd like to get Paul home as soon as possible.'

'It's out front. I'll drive you over.' His glance went beyond her to his cousin just arriving in her wake. 'Unless you'd rather complete the job?'

'No, go ahead,' the other man told him. 'I need a change of clothes. You'll need this,' he added, passing over the suitcase. A hand came out to ruffle Paul's fair hair. ' 'Bye, feller. See you around.' He was gone without a backward glance.

'Let's go,' Gavin invited. 'The architect from Lawson's is due to arrive this weekend, and I want to have everything ready for him.'

So far as Thea knew everything *was* ready—or as much as it could be. The rest was up to the architect himself. Gavin liked to appear up to his neck in it, she acknowledged for the first time. It gave him self-importance. Not an unusual failing, she supposed, and certainly not one to get uptight about. Gavin had weaknesses; well, so did she too. And hers were a great deal harder to stomach.

Nora was overjoyed to see her son again, hugging the wriggling little body with tears in her eyes.

'He looks nearly as well as he used to,' she said, watching him throw his arms about the shaggy mongrel which came bounding into the kitchen. 'Been pining for him, that dog has. I'll have to feed them both up again.'

'The hospital sent a diet sheet,' Thea informed her. 'Dad will bring it over with him after surgery and discuss it with you. Paul's going to be fine.'

Gavin was looking at his watch, obviously anxious to be gone. Back in the car, she asked tentatively, 'Did you want me to come in today?'

He shook his head. 'Leave it till tomorrow. You must have made an early start.' The pause was just long enough to give the question significance. 'Your mother said you were spending the night at a friend of George Yelland's. Were you comfortable?'

'Very.' Thea tried to make her tone light and natural, but knew she had failed when he glanced at her sharply.

'Dave didn't try anything on, did he?'

The jolt of her heart mingled guilt and regret in just about equal amounts. 'Such as what?' she hedged.

'You know what I mean. I've a very good idea he fancies you, and I wouldn't put anything past him.'

'You don't have to worry.' She chose her words carefully, aware that she owed him the truth but unable to bring herself to talk about emotions he wouldn't even be capable of understanding. Gavin didn't have a very strong sex drive; she had known that for a long time without being particularly concerned. Up to meeting Dave she had imagined her own as very little stronger, but he had changed all that. She had wanted him last night, and she still wanted him today. It was a gnawing hunger deep inside her. 'Nothing happened,' she finished on a flat, emotionless note. 'Nothing at all.'

Whether he believed her or not was hard to tell. Certainly he didn't have a lot to say before dropping her off at home.

'See you tomorrow,' he told her through the opened window without bothering to get out of the car. 'I promised Mother I'd stay around tonight. She seems to have gone off Dave.'

Watching the vehicle move off, Thea wished numbly that she could cultivate the same attitude. Being agin Dave was less painful by far than being for him.

The architect arrived on the Saturday and was ac-

commodated at Whirlow. Meeting him for the first time
on Monday morning, Thea was surprised to find him
no older than Gavin, although that was about all they
had in common. Bob Harding was an ambitious young
man with every intention of rising to the top of his
chosen profession.

'I'm seriously considering going overseas,' he confided
in the office one morning, perching on the edge of her
desk. 'There's far more opportunity to get somewhere.'

'I'd have said you were already somewhere,' Thea
returned mildly. Lawson's is one of the biggest builders in
the south.'

His shrug made light of the statement. 'Jobs like this
are small potatoes. I want to be in on the really big
stuff. I was just pipped at the post a couple of months
ago with a design for a block of low-level flats in Exeter.
The planners liked my ideas but didn't consider a one-
man firm could handle the job.'

'And could you have done?' asked Thea.

He grinned. 'With great difficulty. On the other hand,
I could have afforded to take on help with what the job
was worth.'

'Better luck next time,' she sympathised. 'I hope you
find someone willing to take a gamble.'

'Thanks.' He studied her a moment, the eyes behind
the gold-rimmed spectacles curious. 'You know, I've
been wondering——'

'I know,' she said dryly. 'What's a girl like me doing
in a place like this? I've been asked that question before.
The answer is quite simple. It's my home and I happen
to like it.'

He was put neither out nor off. 'Bit dull, I imagine,
though—especially in winter. What on earth do you do
with yourselves?'

'Enough.' Her tone was even. 'It's Midsummer's Day

on Friday, and we make a big occasion of that. Shall you still be here?'

'Probably,' he agreed. 'I'm having some difficulty reconciling what needs doing with the amount of rebuilding the tenants are prepared to tolerate. The older folk are the hardest to convince. I think most of them would rather leave things the way they are.'

Thea laughed. 'I wouldn't be at all surprised. They've lived where they are all their lives and managed quite well. Beyond a certain age I don't suppose new sink units and bathroom suites mean a great deal.'

'Maybe not, but that's what they're getting, among other things. I agree with Barrington. Outside toilets are an ignominy in this day and age. Good idea of his to turn this place into a holiday retreat. Given the right kind of service, a lot of people would pay a great deal to get away from the rat race for a week or two, even if it does mean doing without an en suite bathroom. No reason why we shouldn't be able to fix shower cabinets in each room, though. They're more than large enough to spare an alcove each.'

So Dave really was going to go ahead with his plans for Whirlow. Thea hardly knew whether to be glad or sorry. She wondered if Gavin knew about it yet, and came to the conclusion that he would have mentioned it by now if he did. It was going to be quite a shock both for him and his mother, especially as they would be left holding the fort once Dave went back to South Africa. Somebody should tell him, and soon, yet she hesitated to be the one to do it. Since her return from the mainland their whole relationship had undergone a change. Nothing radical, nothing she could really put a finger on, but there was a difference.

And Dave himself? Well, that was something else again. Sometimes she could almost convince herself there had never been any moments of intimacy between them.

'Penny for them,' said Bob lightly, jerking her abruptly out of her thoughts. Dave's entry at that precise moment brought faint spots of colour to her cheeks. It was almost as if he had been responding to a cue.

'Do you know where Gavin is?' he asked, not stepping beyond the doorway.

'He went down to the hothouses,' she told him. 'Just a routine tour, nothing special.'

'Okay, I'll catch him later.' His glance lifted from her to the man now standing at the side of the desk, mouth taking on a faint slant in the process. 'I wouldn't mind going through the kitchen conversion plans with you while there's nothing else pressing—one or two points Mrs Murray isn't quite happy about.'

'Sure.' The other moved without undue haste. 'Time I stopped interrupting your secretary anyway.' He smiled winningly at Thea. 'Can you let me have those lists by tonight? I need to get them off tomorrow.'

The difficult we do at once, the impossible takes a little longer, Thea thought sourly as the door closed behind the two men. Feeding a clean sheet into the roller, she began to type at her fastest speed, fighting depression in the only way she knew.

Gavin returned some twenty minutes later. Given the message that his cousin had been looking for him, he muttered something under his breath and looked harassed.

'I'll be glad when this whole thing is over and done with!' he exclaimed. 'Where is he now?'

'In the kitchen with Bob.' She hesitated before adding tentatively, 'Are you coming to the meeting tonight, Gavin? I half promised the Vicar we'd handle the White Elephant stall on Friday.'

'Sorry,' he said, not looking at her, 'I shan't be here on Friday. I'm taking Mother to the Lesters' tomorrow, and I shan't be back before Monday. Dave seems willing enough to manage without me.' The last on a faintly bitter note.

It was a moment before she could bring herself to respond. 'Don't you think you could have told me before this?'

'I only knew for sure last night,' he defended. 'Anyway——' he broke off, lifting his shoulders in an apologetic little shrug, 'I can hardly let her go alone.'

Thea failed to see why not, but that wasn't the crucial point right now. She chose to tackle it head on. 'Gavin, are things still the same between us?' she asked. 'I mean, do you still want to marry me?'

His face had changed expression, taking on a wry cast. It took him a little time to answer. 'Yes, I do. I think the question you have to ask yourself is do you want to marry me? No,' as she opened her mouth to speak, 'I don't want you to say anything now. I want you to think about it really hard and seriously, Thea. You have to be sure, otherwise it isn't going to be any use.' He gave her a brief smile and turned back to the door. 'I'll go and find Dave.'

'Gavin,' she said the name softly as he put a hand on the knob, 'I do love you, you know.'

'I know.' He didn't turn round. 'Trouble is I've a feeling I'm closer to a brother than a husband right now.'

She sat without moving for several minutes after he had gone, trying to come to terms with her own emotions. Gavin was right. She had to be sure. If she wanted to marry him she had to put Dave out of her heart and her mind for ever.

Midsummer's Day dawned bright and hot. Too bright

too early, some were heard to murmur, but few paid any heed. By tradition the summer solstice was treated as a general holiday, with everyone out to make the most of it.

In the morning they had the school pageant, this year able to be staged outside on the playground, the playing field having been given over to the Gala itself. Listening to the applause and cries of appreciation drifting across to where she was busy setting up the White Elephant stall, Thea could only surmise that all was going well. Not that it would make a great deal of difference to proud parents if it was a fiasco, she thought fondly. Each and every child on that stage was a star to someone.

'Where do you want this?' asked Bob Harding who had volunteered to take Gavin's place, holding up a particularly hideous green vase. 'Not that it makes any difference, nobody's going to buy it.'

'You'd be surprised,' Thea rejoined lightly, taking it from him. 'Beauty is entirely in the eye of the beholder.'

'Isn't it?' His glance was frankly admiring. 'You know, you're wasted here, Thea. You not only look good, you're good at your job. How about coming and working for me?'

'You already have a secretary,' she reminded him, tongue in cheek. 'A very conscientious one too. Is it six or seven times she's phoned you?'

'Purely in the line of business.' He caught her eye and looked faintly sheepish. 'Well, perhaps not completely. Nothing serious, though.'

'No, well, you can't afford to be, can you?' she said blandly. 'Not if you want to get on. Wives can be such a drag on a man.'

'Coming from someone planning to be one that's no statement to be making,' he observed. 'Or did you change your mind about the joys of marriage?'

'Not noticeably.' There were times when Thea longed for someone in whom she could confide, but Bob was hardly the right person. 'I think those pictures would be better stacked up at the side where people can look through them.'

He accepted the change of subject without demur. 'Will do.'

With less than two hours to go to the official opening, most of the stalls and sideshows were in the final stages of preparation. Looking at the slow build-up of cloud in the east, Thea hoped the weather was going to hold. The pundits had been right, after all, it had been too good a start. Rain was forecast for tomorrow, but the Met people weren't always on the nail. The fate of the barbecue planned for tonight hung in the balance.

Dave put in an appearance at twelve-thirty bearing a tray of cakes and pastries baked by Mrs Murray for the confectionery stall, which was right next door to the White Elephant. He looked amused to see Bob writing out price stickers, strolling across to view the layout with a critical eye.

'Half this stuff must date back before the Flood,' he commented. 'Where on earth do people find it!'

'Some of it has been round more than once,' Thea admitted. She picked out a large earthenware jug. 'This, for instance, has been sold at least six years running to my knowledge. It's porous, apparently. Liquid gradually seeps through it.'

'Then why not get rid of it?'

'The first time it doesn't sell we probably shall. It's a bit of a standing joke to those in the know, you see. Previous owners like to see someone else get caught out.'

He was listening with that mocking tilt to his head, aware as she was that she was talking for the sake of talking. 'Has Gavin contacted you yet?' he asked.

'No.' She schooled herself to sound unconcerned about it. 'There's hardly been time.'

'Not without making it,' he agreed. 'Still, I'm sure they arrived safely.' His gaze moved back to Bob. 'You're definitely leaving us tomorrow?'

'That's right,' answered the younger man. 'I'd have gone today if it hadn't been for this. Couldn't let down a lady in need of help.'

'No, I can see that,' on a dry note. 'I'll fly you over to the mainland in the morning, weather providing.'

'Thanks, I'd appreciate it.' Bob sounded gratified. 'The boat I came over in isn't exactly stable!'

'Thoughtful gesture,' he commented as Dave left. 'Especially with the price of fuel these days. Is he the only pilot on the island?'

'At present,' Thea confirmed. 'He hopes to find one willing to make a base on Sculla permanently.'

'Hey, I might know the very man!' He sounded animated. 'He's been flying for one of the big oil companies in the Gulf for a couple of years, but his wife is expecting their first, so they've come home. Sculla would suit them both right down to the ground. Somewhere safe to bring up a family, and Ray home nights.'

'It sounds ideal. You must discuss it with Dave.' Thea tried to conjure real enthusiasm, failing because acquisition of a pilot could only help bring his eventual departure that much closer. Yet wouldn't it be so much easier when he did go? she asked herself sensibly. Perhaps then she could start picking up the threads of her life again.

The cloud continued to build up during the afternoon, but slowly enough to hold out hope for the evening. By four-thirty most of the stalls were well on the way to being emptied, although the White Elephant still retained a sizeable collection of unsaleable items.

Bob returned from his tea-break wearing what Thea mentally termed a self-satisfied smirk. 'I've got a date for the barbecue,' he announced. 'Blonde, name of Sally. Know her?'

'Of course.' Thea hesitated a moment before adding diffidently, 'She looks older than eighteen, doesn't she?'

'Is that all she is?' He sounded momentarily non-plussed. 'I'd have said at least twenty-two. She came over to me in the refreshment tent. She said she wanted to talk about job prospects in Exeter.'

'She has a job here, if she sticks to it. She's training to be a hairdresser.'

'She could do that in Exeter, I suppose.'

'And live on what?' Thea shook her head. 'Don't en-courage her, Bob. She isn't nearly ready to branch out on her own yet. Fill her head with ideas and you might have her two brothers to deal with—families stick close on Sculla.'

'Okay, you made your point. Nothing to stop me en-joying her company tonight, though, is there?'

Thea could think of at least a couple of the island boys who might consider they had cause to object, but refrained from saying so. At eighteen Sally Anders was old enough to spend the evening with whom she chose.

Dave had not returned to the Gala. She hadn't really expected him to do so, but had found herself keeping an eye out for him anyhow. In all probability he had taken out one of the horses. She could see him in her mind's eye, sitting tall in the saddle, hands light but ready on the reins. Would he be thinking of her at all? Would he remember the first time they had ridden to-gether—the first time he had kissed her? Perhaps fleet-ingly; perhaps even with some regret that he hadn't taken what had been offered that night in Penzance. On the other hand, he might be glad of it. This way he stayed free of involvement.

The Gala finished at five-thirty when people began drifting off home for tea. With the barbecue due to start at seven-thirty it left little time for organisers and helpers to pick up the debris, although the news that the afternoon's takings exceeded two hundred pounds provided a lift.

Arriving home at twenty past seven, Thea seriously contemplated giving the barbecue a miss this year, but habit died hard. Too many people would want to know why, anyway, and tiredness would not be seen as an adequate excuse, especially when she had worked no harder than anyone else this afternoon. Impossible to explain that it was more a weariness of spirit than body. Who would be likely to understand that?

In an effort to do justice to the occasion, she chose a full-skirted dress in a fine white cotton with a drawstring neckline and tiny sleeves, slipping her feet into flat thonged sandals because dancing on grass was hardly compatible with higher heels. A touch of lipstick completed her toilet.

There was going to be a whole lot of curiosity as to why Gavin should have chosen to absent himself from an occasion regarded as one of the highlights of the year, and the excuse of taking his mother to visit friends would hold no more water with others than it had with Thea. It would be assumed they had quarrelled, and speculation as to the cause would be rife—one drawback to living in a close community, she acknowledged, and felt the same sad little sense of loss she had felt before.

CHAPTER EIGHT

THE barbecue was held on the village green in front of the Big Tree. Just about everyone was there when Thea made it, the sheep sizzling on the spit. Most of the older men congregated together drinking island scrumpy and swapping yarns, her father among them—except that in his case the glass in hand was a small one. As the only medical man available he could never afford to be wholly off duty.

Her mother waved a hand from her seat under the oaks where she was ensconced with a dozen or so other wives and mothers keeping a wary eye on younger children while they chatted among themselves. Waving back, Thea had a fleeting glimpse of herself thirty years hence sitting under those self-same trees talking about the self-same island matters, and for the very first time found the idea disquieting. Insular, Dave had called them, and he hadn't been wrong. Sculla was a world all on its own, concerned with little outside of its shores. One had to be of a certain mentality to endure such isolation, and his was not the right kind. She was no longer all that sure of her own any more.

Without Gavin in attendance, she felt very much the odd man out tonight, at least among her own generation. Bob Harding was dancing with Sally Anders, unaware of the glowering regard focussed on him by Rob Cotterill's eldest son, Barry, watching from the sidelines. At twenty-four, Barry was anxious to get himself a wife and start raising a family, Thea knew, but in settling on Sally she privately thought he had taken on rather more than he could handle. Certainly Sally had no intention as yet of settling down with anyone.

Right now she was looking up at Bob with all the provocation she could muster, lips pouting, brows impishly tilted. She was doing it purposely, of course. She knew they were being watched. If there were trouble it was Bob who would be in it, though.

He should be warned, Thea told herself, yet hesitated to do the telling. She doubted if he would take her seriously anyhow.

'Enjoying yourself?' asked an all too familiar voice at her elbow, and she stiffened involuntarily.

'I didn't think you were coming,' she said.

'Why? Because I failed to stay and buy some of your junk this afternoon?'

'The proceeds go towards the children's Christmas party, among other things,' she returned shortly. 'Every little helps.'

Dave took a moment or two in replying. When he did it was on a harder note. 'If it's of any interest, I told Mr Conniston I'd double whatever figure was taken.'

'Dave, I'm sorry.' She caught at his arm as he started to turn away, oblivious to watching eyes. Her own were rueful as she looked up into the hard-hewn features. 'I'm feeling that way out tonight.'

'Missing Gavin?' he suggested.

'Yes.' It was the only answer she could give. 'He's been my partner at the Midsummer barbeque for the last three years.'

'High time you had a change, then.' He made her a mocking little bow. 'Allow me to offer my services.'

Caution fought a brief battle with temptation, and lost. What harm could it do to indulge herself a little so long as she was circumspect? Dave was Gavin's cousin in the eyes of the law. To the islanders that made them

almost as good as brothers. There was nothing more
natural than a man taking care of a future family
member.

'Accepted,' she said, adopting the same light tone, and
knew she deceived neither of them.

It was a good evening, because Dave refused to allow
it to be anything else. When she at one point mentioned
her concern for Bob he promptly drew the other couple
into a foursome, dancing with Sally himself, much to
her unconcealed delight, and suggesting drinks together
afterwards.

Gradually others merged into the group and the sense
of individual couples was lost. Thea saw Dave having a
quiet word with Bob and knew from the expression on
the latter's face that the message had gone home. Sally
might be a very pretty girl, but his interest wasn't deep
enough to risk a punch on the nose from the rejected
suitor, who was appreciably bigger than him.

Served on newly made bread, the roast mutton tasted
delicious. No one bothered with implements, queueing
up to take a portion in their hands and eat it while the
juices still sang.

'The only problem is trying to stop the grease running
down your chin,' Thea complained, wiping hers for the
umpteenth time with the paper napkin provided. 'I'm
going to need a bath before I've finished!'

'You're nibbling it too daintily,' Dave responded on
a jeering note. 'Try being less of the lady and get your
teeth into it. Like this——' tearing off a sizeable chunk
from his own dripping slice.

'Your mouth is bigger than mine,' she retorted, and
dodged the fist he aimed lightly at her chin, her heart
swelling with sudden overwhelming warmth. Forget the
future, she told herself. Concentrate on now—tonight.
Midsummer's Day, a time for magic. Whatever

happened, she was not responsible.

Dusk was closing in fast by the time they finished eating. Lamps were lit and hung from stakes hammered into the ground, and dancing recommenced.

'I feel like taking a walk,' Dave decided, watching the couples moving together. 'Do you want to come?'

'Bored?' Thea queried, and saw a faint smile cross his face.

'Just restless. Every so often I start to feel hemmed in. Africa's a pretty big continent.'

'Yes, I know.' She refused to let the allusion dampen her spirits. 'I'd enjoy a walk.'

She doubted if anyone saw them leave; all were too intent on their own pursuits. They took the path which led up behind the church towards Spring Wood, moving slowly and companionably without talking a great deal. Thea wanted to ask him what he was thinking, but lacked the nerve, knowing he might very well tell her something she shouldn't want to hear. The invitation had not been made on the spur of the moment; he had wanted her alone. In accepting she had been admitting to her own involvement.

The rumble of thunder startled her. In the last few hours she had forgotten all about the threatened rain.

'It's still fairly far away,' said Dave, 'but we'll avoid the woods, just in case.' He took the other branch of the path which eventually finished up at Whirlow, sliding a hand beneath her elbow to guide her footsteps. 'Unless you'd rather turn back now?'

'Would you?' she prevaricated, and felt the hand tighten a little.

'Don't play games,' he said softly. 'It isn't what I brought you out here for.'

She gave him an oblique glance, aware that the moment of truth had come. 'What did you bring me here for, Dave?' she whispered.

The thunder came again before he could answer, closer this time. Before it had fully died away large spots of rain began spattering the ground, heralding a downpour to come.

'We're closer to the house than the village,' Dave stated decisively. 'Can you run?'

She nodded, glad of the flat sandals. 'You go first.'

He put an arm about her shoulders instead, affording some slight protection from the sudden, blinding sting of hail as the heavens opened. With dusk turned to night, Thea had difficulty seeing where she was going, but Dave appeared to have unerring instinct, putting his feet down firmly and without mishap, catching her up when she stumbled and urging her onwards.

It took them only a bare seven or eight minutes to reach Whirlow from the rear, but by that time they were both soaked to the skin. They went in via the small side entrance, pausing to remove muddy shoes in the doorway but still leaving a trail of wet footprints across the carpets.

'First priority is to get out of these things,' said Dave, 'then see about getting them dry.' He sounded matter-of-fact. 'This way.'

Accompanying him up the broad, curving staircase, Thea wondered why the house was so quiet, then remembered that everyone was down at the barbecue. They would be sheltering now, no doubt, unlikely to return until the rain showed some sign of letting up. It gave her a new sense of isolation.

The room to which Dave took her had its own bathroom off. His room, Thea realised, seeing the riding boots standing carelessly by the side of a chest of drawers.

'There's a robe behind the door in there,' he told her.

'Pass me your things out when you get them off and I'll take them down and shove them in the laundry dryer. Have a warm shower. Your rain isn't exactly blood heat.'

'What about you?' she asked, already shivering a little in the wet, clinging garments.

'There are two other bathrooms,' he returned dryly. 'I'll make us some coffee when I go down. Are you going to get those things off?'

She went into the gold and white bathroom and closed the door behind her. All the heady euphoria which had got her into this had flown. She felt not a little ashamed of her behaviour tonight. She had made herself so obvious, so eager for Dave's attentions. If he took advantage of the fact she had only herself to blame.

He was waiting to take the wet clothing from her outstretched hand. 'Coffee in ten minutes or so,' he called.

Her hair lay limp and bedraggled about her face, so wet already it was hardly worth bothering to keep her head out from under the shower. Warmer, but feeling very little better about things, she rubbed it vigorously with a towel until it fluffed out into something approaching its normal style, dreading the moment of Dave's return. The magic was gone, washed out of her by the rain. She wanted desperately to be home—safe in her own bed, her own secure little world. Nothing Dave could offer her equalled that.

She was waiting in the bedroom when he did come, the dark blue robe tightly belted about her waist. It reached her calves, enveloping her snugly. She caught the faint elusive scent of his aftershave every time she moved her head.

Clad in jeans and a thin cotton sweater, he looked fully in command of himself. 'Your dress is almost dry,' he announced, handing her a mug from the tray he had brought with him. 'You might like to run a warm iron over it before you put it on. The creases don't drop out of cotton.'

She circled the mug in her hands, trying for a light note. 'I didn't realise you were so domesticated.'

'A bachelor has to be. I don't carry much of a house staff. Most of my stuff goes to the laundry, but I'm not above rinsing through a shirt on occasion.'

'Is your house very big?'

'Moderately—just the one storey. Most South African homesteads are.' He had seated himself on the edge of the double bed a few feet from her chair, face closed against her. 'My father built the place when he first bought the land, so it has a lot of English notions incorporated—including the furnishings. He had the lot shipped out.'

'You sound disapproving,' Thea commented.

'Only of the general idea. Untreated British woods don't stand up to our climate too well—frames warp. I've had to get rid of a lot of pieces he set store by. Eventually just about everything will have to be changed.'

'Then you can forget your English side altogether.' She hadn't meant to say it, but now it was out she felt the need to continue. 'You never had any intention of staying on Sculla, did you?'

'Not once I'd seen what it had to offer,' he admitted. The grey eyes were direct. 'I could never live the kind of life you live here.'

But I could live yours, she had the sudden wild impulse to say! Instead she heard herself asking calmly, 'Is there so much difference?'

'Yes. I tried to persuade myself there wasn't, but there comes a point where it's no use pretending any longer.

This place is like Shangri-la—beautiful, but boring. You all of you lack any semblance of normal curiosity or ambition.'

'Zombies, you mean.'

'That isn't what I said. Where people live without stress or challenge of any kind the intellect becomes dulled. They stop thinking or feeling about anything with any great depth. Young Sally's the only one I've met with any yen to get out and make a different kind of life for herself—perhaps because subconsciously she recognises that if she stays here she'll become like the rest of you.'

'Perhaps she's the one you should concern yourself with then. The rest of us are obviously beyond redemption.' Thea got up and replaced the mug on the tray with shaking fingers, too torn inside to take any more. 'Why don't you just go on back where you came from, Dave? We never wanted you here in the first place.'

It was a moment before he answered, voice controlled. 'What I said just now doesn't apply to the way I feel about you personally. You have to realise that.'

'Oh, I do!' She had swung to face him, eyes blazing in the angry pallor of her face. 'After all, it isn't my mind you're interested in, is it! You know, in former times the lord of any English manor had first claim on any bride. You'd have been in your element then!'

'You're no bride,' he pointed out on a dangerously quiet note. 'And you wanted the same thing not so very long ago.'

'Midsummer madness,' she flung at him. 'That's all it was. You could no more make me feel that way again than fly!'

The sudden purposeful set of his jaw was all the warning he gave. He had hold of her before she was fully aware of his movement, jerking back her head so that she looked straight into the leaping grey eyes. 'There's one sure way of disproving that,' he stated.

His mouth was bruising, cutting off her breath, yet it struck an immediate core of response. She tried to stop him taking off the robe that was her only covering, but she couldn't, her hands suddenly nerveless. Then he was holding her away from him to look at her, and his expression was changing, the anger giving way to something infinitely more disturbing.

His fingers traversed the length of her body, tracing the curve of hip and waist with a touch so light she could scarcely bear the torment. He didn't speak, just lifted her up and carried her to the bed, laying her down and pressing his lips once to each breast before straightening again. It took him bare moments to shed his own clothing, then he was back with her, his hand seeking her hips to pull her closer to him as he kissed her long and hard.

She responded without restraint, her emotions totally committed. Gavin no longer mattered; nothing else mattered but this moment, this man. She wanted to give him everything, to experience everything. She loved him, she knew that now. Loved him enough to damn the future.

There was pain when he came into her, but not for long. She cried his name once at the end when all control was stripped from her, sliding down, down, down into a world from which she never wanted to emerge.

It was a long time before Dave moved, rolling on to his back to lie gazing at the ceiling.

'You're not going to believe it,' he said on a low, rough note, 'but I never intended that to happen.'

Well, what had she expected? Thea asked herself numbly. Words of love? A proposal of marriage? She had asked for everything she had got.

'You're right,' she said, deliberately hardening her voice, 'I don't believe it. You knew when you brought me here just what was going to happen. You planned every minute of it!'

'Did I plan the rain too?' He made a swift move back to her as she started to sit up, holding her down so that he could look into her face, his own rueful. 'You're not going anywhere till you've heard me out.'

'There's nothing to say.' She was trembling, striving for control over her emotions. 'You did what you set out to do. That's all there is to it.'

His jaw hardened a little. 'I didn't exactly have to rape you.'

'I know.' She refused to turn her head away, forcing herself to meet his eyes. 'You get ten out of ten for effort. Congratulations.'

'Thea, stop it!' The rueful quality was back. 'We have to talk this out.'

'No!' Her control was slipping, bit by bit. 'I hate postmortems. It happened and that's it.'

'But you still believe I planned it this way?'

'Yes,' she said flatly.

'Then you're right, there isn't anything more to be said.' Face closed, he got up and reached for his jeans, pulling them on. 'I'll fetch you your things.'

Thea forced herself on to her feet as soon as he left, going into the bathroom and locking the door behind her. Her face in the mirror looked drained, her eyes dark and bruised. 'Tramp,' she said out loud, and meant it. What she had done had been for purely self-indulgent reasons, because she had known it would mean little to Dave. He had made no pretences, either before or after.

So where to go from here? she wondered. Not back to Gavin, for certain. He deserved better. What she would tell him she had no idea. Anything, she supposed, but the truth. She didn't want to face that herself.

Dave made no attempt to come into the bathroom when he came back, knocking once on the door. 'They're out here when you want them,' he said. 'I'm going to get the car out.'

The white dress was, as he had warned her, creased and wrinkled. Thea pulled it on without glancing in the mirror, looking for her sandals before remembering that they were still down in the side lobby. Dave came in through the main entrance as she descended the stairs, the cotton sweater spotted on the shoulders with rain.

'It's letting up,' he announced, 'but the drive is waterlogged. One of the drains must have blocked up.' He crossed to a cupboard let into the panelling and took out a light raincoat. 'Put this round your shoulders. No point in getting wet again.'

The rain had lessened considerably from what it had been but was still fairly heavy. Thea slid her feet into the sandals Dave had fetched through from the lobby, and ran with him down the steps to the car he had parked as close as he could get it. He was damper than ever by the time he got round to the driver's side, but he didn't seem to care overmuch. There was a look about his mouth that discouraged any solicitous comment, even if she had felt like making it.

He didn't speak once on the way, concentrating on the dark narrow roadway. The village was quiet when they went through it, the green forlorn and abandoned. There was a light still on in the front bedroom of the doctor's house. Thea could imagine her mother lying there listening to the sound of the car—if she had gone to bed at all. They would know she had been with Dave; they couldn't fail to know. What they mustn't ever learn was the rest of it.

He leaned across her to open the door the moment

the car came to a stop. 'Home,' he said. 'It's what you wanted, isn't it?'

'Yes.' She started to get out, freezing as his hand touched the nape of her neck. 'Don't!'

'I was turning up your coat collar,' he said, 'not dragging you back into the car.' He sounded weary. 'Thea, I'm sorry it happened the way it did, but having said that I'm not going to spend any more time apologising. Tomorrow we start sorting ourselves out.'

'If we do it will be separately,' she stated, and got out of the car, closing the door in his face.

He waited until she had opened the gate before moving off. Listening to the fading sound of the engine, she felt totally and utterly alone.

Margaret Ralston appeared at the head of the stairs as she went indoors. She was in her dressing gown.

'We were worried about you,' she said. 'Do you realise it's almost midnight?'

'No, I didn't,' Thea admitted with perfect truth. 'We got caught in the rain, and Dave took me back to Whirlow to dry out. I'm sorry, I should have phoned down.'

'Yes, you should.' Her mother hesitated, searching her face, as she came up the stairs towards her. 'What made you go off with Dave in the first place?'

'We both felt like a walk.' Thea wondered at her ability to sound so casual about it. 'He wanted to talk about Whirlow. He's planning on turning the place into a kind of vacational rest home for weary mainlanders. After he's gone, of course.'

'He's leaving Sculla?'

'That's right. He never intended to stay, it turns out.' Her smile was brittle. 'Gavin did all that worrying for nothing. Everything is going to be the way it was before. Apart from the visitors, that is. I daresay we'll get used to them in time.'

'Gavin rang you here tonight about half an hour ago,' her mother said. 'He had something important to tell you. I had to tell him you weren't home yet. He's phoning back first thing in the morning.'

'Then I'd better get to bed, hadn't I, or I'm not going to be awake when he does.' Thea smiled again, apologetically this time. 'I was thoughtless.'

'So was Dave.' It was apparent that there were other questions she would have liked to ask, but she held them back. 'That dress is a mess, you'd better put it out for the wash.'

'I will,' Thea promised. ' 'Night, Mom.'

Alone at last in her own room, she prepared for bed like an automaton, sliding between the sheets to lie gazing into the darkness with sleep a million light years away. Her body felt tense, pulsing with new-found hunger, longing for the touch of hands she knew she would never feel again. Loving a man wasn't enough when he didn't love her back. She had learned that the hard way. Just let the lesson sink well in.

CHAPTER NINE

GAVIN telephoned at eight-thirty, his voice clear on the line. 'Where were you last night?' he demanded almost immediately. 'It wasn't far off midnight when I phoned. I deliberately left it until I thought the barbecue would be over.'

'We were rained off,' she said. 'I suppose Mom told you. I had to take shelter until it eased up.'

'Where?'

'At Whirlow.' There was no point in trying to hide it. She carried on before he could speak. 'Did you know Dave was definitely going back to South Africa?'

The pause was long and weighted. 'No, I didn't,' he admitted at length. 'He hasn't said anything to me.'

'He only told me because I asked him outright.' Thea waited a moment before going on. 'Gavin, you realise what this means? You'll be Master of Sculla again.'

'Only nominally. Dave can only delegate, he can't turn over.'

'Does that matter so much?'

'Yes, it matters.' His tone was brusque. 'Especially now.'

'Why now?' she asked. 'What happened?'

'I've been offered another job—some American friends of the Lesters. They've just bought an estate on the mainland about thirty miles from here and want a reliable agent to run it for them. Nowhere near the size of Sculla, of course, but there are three home farms, and they're going to breed their own beef herd.'

'You don't know anything about cattle,' she said blankly.

'I don't need to, not in that sense. I'd be dealing with the marketing side, that's all. The point is, there's a house all ready with the job—the old Lodge. Needs a little work on it, but the Partons will see to all that. Mother's enthusiastic. She could have her own flat in Gloucester, and be within easy reach of friends and family. They've agreed to pay me the same salary I was drawing from Whirlow to start, with increments according to performance. Couldn't be fairer than that.'

Thea's mind felt numb. What did she say? What did he expect her to say?

'It sounds an excellent proposition,' she got out at last. 'Are you seriously considering it?'

'I've accepted it.' There was a faint note of apology in the statement. 'I had Sculla handed to me on a platter, Thea. This job I got on my own merits by proving I knew what I was talking about.'

'You must have been busy,' she said weakly.

'Yes, I have. The Lesters had it all planned for me to meet the Partons on Thursday evening, and yesterday I spent going over the estate with Jeff Parton. You'd like him—you'd like them both. They'll only be over here part of the year. They've a place in California too.' He paused, voice lacking in vitality when he came on again. 'You don't want to leave Sculla?'

'It isn't that so much.' Thea hardly knew how to put it. 'Gavin, remember what we talked about the other day before you left? More of a brother and sister relationship, you said. Do you really think that's any real basis for marriage?'

'I was jealous,' he admitted. 'I knew you were attracted to Dave.'

'And now you think you made a mistake?'

'No, but I've got things into better perspective. Dave is a passing fancy. We go back a long time. It takes more than a simple attraction to make a marriage work.'

Her voice was soft. 'Does this job of yours depend on you having a wife?'

It took him a moment or two to answer. When he did it was with his usual dependable honesty. 'It isn't essential, just preferred. I shan't lose it if I stay a bachelor. They've had enough trouble finding the right man.'

'Good.' She paused, reluctant to make it final over the phone. 'Can we talk about it when you get back?'

'If necessary.' He sounded depressed, as if he already knew what the answer was going to be. 'It might have been better if I'd waited to tell you the whole thing when I get back.'

Amen to that, she thought, remembering the possible listener down at the Post Office switchboard. Not that it made a great deal of difference in the long run; people were going to have to know sooner or later.

'See you on Monday, then,' said Gavin. 'Don't bother telling Dave, I'd rather like to do it myself.'

One could hardly grudge him that satisfaction, Thea reflected, putting down the receiver. Dave was going to be left with a problem. Who would he leave in charge of Sculla now? Useless hoping that he might decide to stay himself. He had made his feeling on that score too painfully clear. It made little difference where she was concerned anyway.

The weather was cooler but bright after the rain. Thea rode over to the northernmost point of the island and spent the day beachcombing, lonely as she had never been. Dave found her there at three in the afternoon.

'I've been over just about the whole island looking for you,' he said, dismounting from Major. 'We have to talk, Thea.'

'About what?' she asked, not even glancing up from the small pile of objects she had gathered together. 'See this?' indicating a half rotted name plate. '*Sea Wanderer*. I wonder how long ago she went down? It should be possible to find out.'

'Did it occur to you that you might be pregnant?' he demanded with blunt deliberation, and this time gained the required response, a small grim smile touching his lips as her head jerked upright. 'I'm taking it for granted there is a chance?'

'I suppose there is.' Her voice was unsteady. Why hadn't she thought of it? 'I don't take the pill.'

'With your father the only one available to prescribe it, it might have been difficult even if you'd considered it,' he agreed. 'I should have thought about it.'

'Knowing how naïve I was about such things?' She looked at him with veiled green eyes. 'Would it have stopped you?'

Dave shook his head, expression rueful. 'Not the way things were. I was past thinking about anything.'

'Flattering to think I have such a devastating effect!'

He bent suddenly and shook her by the shoulders, drawing her upright and holding her there, fingers burning her flesh. 'Don't play the cynic for me!'

'Do you hold a monopoly?' she flashed. 'Don't worry, Dave, if it did turn out that way I shouldn't be making any claims on you!'

His eyes narrowed. 'You wouldn't consider abortion, I hope.'

It wouldn't have entered her head, no matter how desperate her situation, but she was in no mood to give him that assurance. 'What else would you suggest—

marrying me out of hand?'

There was a lengthy pause before he answered, expression as unreadable as only he could make it. 'If I asked you would you do it?'

The jerk of her heart was sickening in more senses than one. She wanted to hurt him physically—to reach out and rake her nails down his unheeding face. 'I wouldn't marry you,' she said with icy clarity, 'for anything in the world!'

His eyes were steely. 'You might feel differently about that in a few weeks' time.'

'You mean you intend hanging on long enough to find out?'

'My departure was never that imminent. I'll be here till the end of the summer.'

Thea looked at him blindly, fighting to conceal the emotions running riot inside her. 'You don't owe me anything. As you said, I wanted it too.'

'You wanted what I'd taught you to want,' he responded. 'I intended opening your eyes just far enough to see what might be missing from your relationship with Gavin, only it got out of hand. Whatever happens now, I'm responsible.'

'Then you can rest easy, because nothing is going to happen.'

'You can't be sure of that.'

'But I am.' She was working hard to convince them both. 'Call it feminine intuition.'

The smile came again, no less grim. 'You're not *that* naïve. I'll be watching you, Thea. You won't be able to hide anything from me. I wouldn't trust you not to do something desperate if it does happen.'

She was silent, not trusting herself to speak. He let her go, turning away to take hold of Major's rein close up by the bit. 'Are you ready to go back?'

'No,' she said. 'Not with you. If you stay on Sculla I'll leave myself!'

'Telling your parents what?' He shook his head. 'You can't run away from it. If you try I'll have you traced.'

'As another man's wife I'd be his responsibility, not yours,' she responded tautly, and saw his expression undergo an abrupt alteration.

'You don't have it in you to cheat Gavin into marrying you ahead of schedule.'

'I shouldn't attempt to cheat him. I'd tell him everything first.'

'And you really believe he'd accept it, just like that?'

'Yes.' Her head was flung back, her face set in lines of defiance. 'He'll understand because he's the kind of man he is—the kind you couldn't even begin to emulate. As for the time factor, he already wants to bring the wedding forward. He rang me only this morning to talk about it.'

The lean features revealed little. 'Why should he do that?'

'Ask him when he comes back,' she flashed. 'He'll be only too pleased to tell you.'

'*You* tell me.'

'No.' Despite herself she took a step backwards out of reach of his grasp. 'He wants to do it himself.'

Dave came after her purposefully, leaving Major to look after himself. The long fingers dug into bone. 'I said *you* tell me! Or do I have to shake it out of you?'

'Even in my possible condition?' she mocked, and knew she had gone too far even before she saw his eyes flame.

Last night he had carried her to bed, this time he carried her to the dunes a hundred yards away, holding her under him until she stopped struggling.

'Once might be explained away,' he said softly, face close to hers. 'Twice is something else again. Do you want me to show you how easy it would be?'

She moved her head in brief negation, too well aware of her own weaknesses. If her mind said no, her body was already saying yes. He wouldn't have to try too hard to conquer her better instincts.

'Then tell me,' he said.

She did so briefly and succinctly, hating herself for letting Gavin down this way. 'So now you're going to have to find a new manager as well as a pilot,' she finished, not bothering to conceal the vindictive note in her voice. 'I wish you joy of it!'

'The pilot won't be any problem. Bob Harding told me about this friend of his when I took him over this morning. I already arranged a meeting.' Dave sounded remarkably unmoved by the news. 'And I've got a couple of months to do something about the other. As a job for a family man it holds out excellent prospects. I doubt if I'll have any trouble finding someone reliable.' He was looking at her mouth inches below his, his eyes holding an expression she recognised. When he moved it was abruptly, sitting up to run a hard hand through his hair before coming to rest with elbows supported on bent knees. 'I won't let you do it, Thea!'

'If it's what Gavin wants you can't stop me.' She almost whispered the words, knowing they went against every instinct in her. 'You can't claim rights over something you're not even sure exists.'

'Rights?' His laugh came short. 'Do you think I want you to be pregnant? Marry Gavin and you could be ruining his life as well as your own. If you have any feeling at all for him you won't even give him the chance to be understanding.'

There was a tight dryness in her throat, a misery so deep it threatened to choke her. Of course she couldn't marry Gavin. She had known that from the start. Forgive her though he might, she couldn't put him in that kind of spot.

'Why did you have to come here?' she demanded bitterly. '*You* ruined *my* life!'

'I realise it.' His voice was rough. 'That's why I'm trying to put things right now.'

'By offering to marry me if it turns out to be necessary?' The irony seared.

He said it without turning his head. 'So marry me anyway.'

In the sudden stillness the cries of the gulls hovering on the wind seemed to echo her feelings. Thea wanted to scream at him the same way, to pound those broad, unfeeling shoulders with her fists. 'Go to the devil!' she got out through clenched teeth, and scrambled to her feet, looking round wildly for Lady.

The mare was grazing some distance away beyond the narrow stretch of dunes. Thea picked up the saddle she had left stashed in a hollow on the way to get her. Catching her up as she reached the animal, Dave took the saddle from her to sling it over the silky back.

'I don't need your help,' she gritted. 'Get away from her!'

'I don't think you know what you need,' he said, reaching for the girths. 'Apart from last night. We could build on that.'

She had stopped protesting because it was useless, standing by while he cinched up, fists clenched at her sides. 'Where? South Africa?'

'Here to start with. We'd still spend the summer.' He let down the flap and gave the mare a brisk slap on the withers, causing her to sidestep as he turned back to look at Thea with taut composure. 'I can promise you a pretty good life style out there. With Karen Ryall for a neighbour you'd never be short of a friend.'

'Keep your promises for someone who might appreciate them,' she retorted, snatching the rein from him. 'I'm not interested!'

'So we'll wait and see what transpires.'

'It won't make any difference.'

'It will if it turns out you're carrying my child,' he came back hardily. 'I'd say the chances were pretty even. Think about it, Thea.'

She didn't want to think about it, the possibility was too real. The old values still applied on Sculla. Her mother would die of shame.

Swinging herself up into the saddle, she turned Lady's head for home, conquering the urge to break into a gallop because she knew Dave would only catch her up. She supposed she should feel grateful for his concern on a point to which most men would prefer to turn a conveniently blind eye, but she couldn't bring herself to feel anything of the kind. If she married him now or, heaven forbid, later, nothing would ever be clear between them.

It would be nearly three weeks before she could count on any evidence to set her mind at rest, she calculated. Three weeks of wondering and waiting and hoping against hope. She couldn't burden Gavin with that kind of problem; he had enough of his own.

Dave came up with her but didn't speak. He had, she acknowledged, already said all there was to say. Oh God, she thought numbly, feeling his thigh brush hers as the horses came momentarily together, why couldn't it have been different?

The *Molly* docked promptly at nine on Monday evening under a sky rimmed with pure gold from the setting sun. Waiting on the quayside, Thea saw Gavin come on deck from the direction of the saloon, and lifted an arm to wave a greeting until she realised he wasn't looking her way but back the way he had come, extending a hand to assist someone out of the hatch.

A girl, she saw: tall, dark and very attractive even from here. She was laughing as she came into view, her hand still lying in Gavin's, who seemed in no hurry to release it. When he did it was only to bend and lift not one but two suitcases from the deck, moving towards the gangway in the company of his new-found friend.

He spotted Thea as he reached the quayside, making some comment to the girl at his back before swinging in her direction.

'I wasn't sure you'd be here,' he said, bending to kiss her lightly on the cheek. He put down the cases and turned to the girl standing a little distance away, beckoning her closer. 'Blaire Westwood, Thea Ralston. Thea's father is the doctor here.'

'Hi there.' The other had a deep, almost masculine voice—the kind many would call sexy—and an intonation Thea recognised instantly.

'You're South African!' she exclaimed.

The wide, mobile mouth broke into a smile. 'Is it that obvious?'

'It's apparent.' Thea had a sense of foreboding. 'Are you a friend of Dave's?'

Blaire laughed, sounding genuinely amused. 'You could call it that. Is he here?'

'Not at the moment.' Thea paused. 'You're expected?'

'No, I wanted to surprise him. I've been in the States

for a few months. His letter saying he was coming here only caught up with me a couple of weeks ago. I planned on seeing something of England before I went back home, so it seemed an ideal opportunity to make a small detour.' She laughed again, wryly this time. 'That boat must be flat-bottomed. I don't think I ever came as close to being sea-sick in my life!'

'You're not on your own,' Gavin put in with hearty feeling. 'If Dave had known you were coming I'm sure he'd have come over in the helicopter to fetch you.'

'You've got a 'copter here? That's good news. He uses one back home, of course. Needs it to get from property to property.'

'You mean there's more than one?' It was Gavin who asked the question, surprise unconcealed. 'He never mentioned that.'

'He's into wattle as well as fruit, although Whirlow is his main base.'

Thea said quietly, 'That's the same name as the house here.'

'Really? Well, his father always did have this nostalgic streak.' Blaire looked about her a little restlessly. 'How do we get to the house?'

'Dad let me have his car,' Thea said to Gavin. 'He isn't expecting any calls tonight. I'm probably the smallest, so I'll go in the back, if you'd like to drive. It isn't very big,' she added for Blaire's benefit, 'or very new, but it will get us where we want to go. This way.'

The South African walked beside her along the quayside, leaving Gavin to bring up the rear with the suitcases. She was about twenty-five, twenty-six, Thea guessed, and possessed of a confidence which made her feel gauche. The linen slacks and matching safari-style jacket were superbly cut, the silky shirt beneath opened at the throat on a scarlet neckerchief casually knotted.

'Have you known Dave long?' she heard herself asking, already knowing the answer.

'Oh, all my life. We're next-door neighbours, although my place isn't on the same scale. I can't wait to get back, though I wouldn't have missed this trip. Dave was right to suggest it. It seems years since I saw him, How is he? When does he plan on going home?'

'He's fine,' Thea assured her dully. 'You'll have to ask him about the other.'

They had only just reached the little old Morris when the only other vehicle on the island came down the road from the village to pull to an abrupt stop beside the group. Dave got out slowly from behind the wheel, leaning an arm along the top of the door to gaze in blank astonishment at the newcomer.

'Blaire?' he exclaimed. 'How on earth——'

'Spur of the moment, darling.' She went across and kissed him, arms sliding about his neck with tell-tale familiarity. 'Pleased?'

He made no attempt to disengage himself from the embrace, looking down at her with an odd little smile on his lips. 'I might be when I've got over the shock. Where the devil did you spring from?'

'London. I landed this morning and took a train straight down to—Penzance, is it?' She was laughing, not in the least put out by the apparent lack of enthusiasm in his greeting. 'You know, it took *hours* to even find out how to get here, and then I finish up in an old tub like that one. If it hadn't been for Gavin I'd have thrown myself overboard halfway across!'

'You always did exaggerate.' A hand touched the side of her face in a gesture that made Thea's heart ache.

'Good to see you.' To Gavin he added, 'I'll take Blaire up, you come with Thea. I'm sure the two of you have a lot to talk about. Sling the cases in the back here, there's more room.'

Following the other car up through the village, Thea asked tentatively, 'How long do you have before you take up your new job?'

'A month,' Gavin said. 'Long enough for Dave to find himself a new agent. There's little wonder he wasn't keen on staying here with someone like Blaire waiting for him back home!'

'Not exactly waiting,' Thea murmured.

'You know what I mean.' He gave her a swift, sideways glance. 'Does it hurt to know he has a woman of his own?'

'No.' There was no way she could tell the truth. 'Like you said, it was just a passing fancy.'

'Good.' He sounded relieved. The next question was a little longer in coming. 'Have you thought about what I said, Thea?'

She gave a small, inaudible sigh. 'I've thought about it.'

'And?' he prompted.

'I'm sorry.' She said it with sincerity and not a little unhappiness. 'I can't marry you, Gavin. It wouldn't work out.'

'Why?' he demanded. 'Just tell me why? You said you loved me.'

'I do. It's not the right kind of love, that's all.' She was trying to stay unemotional about it and barely succeeding. 'Gavin, try to understand. It's best for you as well as me. You'll find someone else.'

'And who will you find?' His tone was cool, hiding his hurt. 'Dave is already spoken for.'

'I know.' She attempted to make light of it. 'Perhaps

the new agent will turn out to be my type.'

'*I'm* your type,' he burst out, losing his composure. 'Thea, stop the car. How the devil can we sort this out while you're driving!'

'There's nothing to sort out,' she insisted, beginning to feel desperate. 'You have to accept it as final, Gavin. I'm sorry, truly sorry, but that's the way it is.'

'It's Dave I blame,' he said bitterly after a moment or two. 'Before he came you were perfectly happy.'

'I thought I was. Now I realise we were just marking time.' She kept her eyes front, driving slowly because the road ahead was so dim and narrow. 'I have to get away too. I'm not sure where and when, but it's time I did something different.'

'Your parents aren't going to like that idea.'

She bit her lip. 'I realise that. On the other hand, it isn't as if I'd never be seeing them again.'

Gavin shook his head. 'I can hardly believe so much could change in less than a month.'

'But you're looking forward to your new job, aren't you?'

'Yes.' He brightened just a little. 'Yes, I am.'

Whirlow was in sight, lights welcoming against the encroaching dusk. The car ahead had already parked, its occupants vanished indoors. Thea brought the Morris to a stop, sitting still as Gavin got out and came round the rear of the car.

'Aren't you coming in?' he asked.

'Not now,' she said. 'There isn't really much point.' Her smile was forced. 'See you in the morning.'

She was home before ten, finding her father making himself a bedtime drink in the kitchen.

'Your mother had a bad head and went to bed early,' he said. 'I didn't expect you back for some time yet.'

'I felt like an early night myself,' she prevaricated. 'Is there enough milk in there for two?'

'If there isn't I can always top up with water.' John Ralston took down another mug from the rack and spooned cocoa powder into it, added liquid to fill the two mugs and brought both of them across to the table where Thea had taken a seat.

'Now supposing we talk about what's bothering you,' he said quietly, sitting down opposite her. 'And don't try saying nothing, because we'll both know it isn't true. You've been on edge all weekend.'

Meeting the familiar, kindly eyes, Thea knew a sudden strong temptation to let go and tell him the whole truth. He was a doctor. Perhaps there were ways of telling even this early whether or not she was pregnant. The feeling passed almost immediately. She couldn't do it. Why destroy his peace of mind as well as her own? She had to settle for half the truth and hope it would satisfy him.

'I'm sorry,' she said. 'I should have told you. Gavin is leaving Sculla for a job on the mainland.'

'You mean it's already definite?' He sounded perturbed. 'That was rather sudden.'

'Yes, it was. The first I knew about it was when he phoned on Saturday morning. I suppose it was too good an opportunity to miss.'

'But surely you told him Dave wouldn't be staying on Sculla?'

'Yes, of course I did. It didn't make any difference. I think he just wants to get right away from the Barrington name. The new job starts in a month.'

Her father looked down at his mug without attempting to lift it to his lips. 'And he naturally wants you to go with him. Well, I can't pretend it won't be a wrench losing you, but that has to come second to your happiness. What do you plan to do—bring the wedding forward?'

'No.' Her voice was unsteady. 'I don't want to marry him at all. Not any more.'

The greying head came up, his eyes searching her face. 'Because of this job?'

'It's more than that.' She spread her hands ruefully. 'I made a mistake. I don't love him the way I should.'

Her father looked at her for a long moment, expression slowly changing. 'Which way should you love him?'

'More deeply,' she said. 'More—oh, I can't really put it into words. Just more.'

'More like the way you feel about Dave, perhaps?' He gave a faint smile at the look in her eyes. 'I'm not blind, neither is your mother. We've both of us seen the change in you since he came to Sculla, although we hoped it was just a temporary attraction.' He hesitated briefly. 'Does he feel the same way about you, by any chance?'

'No.' There was little point in prevarication. Her own smile was wry. 'As a matter of fact, a girl-friend of his turned up on the *Molly* tonight. Well, rather more than just a girl-friend, I suppose. She's from Natal.'

'I'm sorry.' The sympathy was real enough, but it was mingled with relief. 'Still, it's perhaps for the best. He's not of our world, Thea.'

'I know.' She could say that with conviction. 'And don't worry about it. I'll get over him.' Never, another part of her mind stated just as firmly, but she ignored it. Providing nothing came of her fears she would make herself forget him. 'What I'd really like to do,' she added purely on impulse, 'is go and stay with Aunt Thelma in Exeter for a week or two until I get myself sorted out. Do you think she would have me?'

'I'm sure of it. And I think it's a good idea. You
might lose your job, though. Dave would have to get
someone else in. More especially so with all the work
going on.'

'I'd have to worry about that later.' She added diffidently, 'Would you phone Aunt Thelma and do the
asking for me, Dad? She's more likely to be honest about
it with you.'

'Of course. First thing tomorrow.' He reached across
and put his hand to her cheek in tender understanding.
'It would have to happen this way. Pity Dave didn't see
it himself and take steps to counteract it. He's astute
enough.' He paused, registering some flicker of expression across her face. 'He didn't go the other way and
deliberately encourage you, I hope?'

The answer to that, she supposed, had to be yes, but
she had no intention of destroying any more illusions. 'I
didn't need encouragement, I'm afraid.' She gave him a
reassuring smile. 'I'll get over him. I just need to get
away.'

'And so you shall. I'll explain to your mother. I can't
promise she won't be upset, but she'll realise it's for the
best. What about tomorrow? Are you going in to
work?'

'I have to,' she said. 'I can't walk out on the job at a
moment's notice. I'll go to Exeter on Saturday, if that
suits Aunt Thelma.' She drained the mug of cocoa and
got up. 'I'm shattered.'

'You'll feel better after a good night's sleep,' he
agreed. 'Goodnight, chick.'

Why on earth had she said she'd go to Exeter? Thea
asked herself as she went upstairs. Her aunt was well-
meaning, but she would naturally be curious as to why
her brother's daughter should suddenly take it into her
head to pay a lengthy visit after all this time. Living

with the Rourke family had not been all that easy before, and she doubted if Cousin Jenny and she would have very much more in common now.

The answer, of course, was obvious. She had to go somewhere and it was the only place to go. To spend the next three weeks or so seeing Dave every day would be more than she could bear. If the worst came to the worst she wasn't sure how she would tackle it. She didn't want to consider that aspect unless she had to.

CHAPTER TEN

THE following couple of days were among the longest Thea had ever known. She saw Dave only infrequently, and then only in the company of others. Blaire was unfailingly pleasant, but there seemed to be an aloofness about her that had not been there on her arrival. At lunchtime Thea would sometimes sense the other girl eyeing her appraisingly across the table as if trying to weigh something up, but that was as far as it went. If the South African harboured any suspicions at all, she was keeping them to herself.

It was Wednesday afternoon before Thea finally had the opportunity to speak to Dave alone, when he came to the office while Gavin was out.

'I know it's customary to ask for holiday entitlements in advance,' she said formally, 'but I'd like to start mine this coming Saturday. I have three weeks due for the year.'

He studied her for a moment before replying, face austere. 'I don't think you can be spared right now,' he said at length. 'The builders will be here on Monday.'

'You don't seem to understand.' She was looking at the half completed letter in her machine, not at him. 'I'm going, Dave. If you want to call my employment terminated you'll have to do it.'

'Going where?' he asked, ignoring the rest.

'To an aunt's on the mainland.'

'Until you know which way things are going to work out?' He sounded curt. 'No dice.'

Her head came up, green eyes meeting grey on a swift

flare of anger. 'You can't stop me!'

'I can,' he stated with wholly believable certainty. 'And I will, if necessary—even if it means telling your parents the whole story.'

Thea stared at him, her heart even now reacting to the memory of those moments she had spent in his arms. 'Why?' she asked huskily.

'Because I want you where I can keep an eye on you.'

'You still don't trust me not to do something stupid, do you?' She shook her head with emphasis. 'There's no way I'd do what you're thinking, even if I knew where to go.'

'It's still the same answer.'

She drew in a long, slow breath, fighting for the control she needed. 'Why did you have to mention the possibility at all?' she asked bitterly. 'I'd probably never have thought about it if you hadn't.'

Something flickered in the grey eyes. 'If you're prepared for the worst it doesn't hit as hard if it comes. Believe me, there'll be no one more relieved than I shall if it turns out the right way.'

'Yes,' she said with deliberation, 'it would be rather difficult to explain away to Blaire, wouldn't it?'

There was no reaction that she could see in his face. 'Blaire doesn't enter into it.'

'You mean she went to all this trouble to see you for no particular reason.' She moved her head in repudiation. 'I'm not an idiot, Dave. I saw the way she greeted you—the way you reacted. Don't try telling me there's never been anything between you.'

'I'm not going to try telling you anything,' he said. 'Right now it wouldn't be any use.' He waited a moment before adding on a different note, 'I take it you've finally shed Gavin.'

'Finally and irrevocably,' she agreed. 'You were right.

When it came to the point, I couldn't put him in that kind of spot.'

Dave's mouth slanted. 'One less bridge to cross. Now all we have to do is wait.'

'It won't make any difference,' she said. 'No matter what happens.'

'Tell me that if it does, and I might believe you.' He picked up the plan he had come to fetch, added levelly, 'Remember, Thea, no running away. Your father and I have a good relationship—I'd hate to disillusion him unnecessarily.'

She was still sitting slumped in her chair when Gavin came back some fifteen minutes later. He eyed her with concern. 'Are you all right?' he asked.

She nodded, forcing herself to sit up. 'Just tired. I haven't been sleeping too well lately.'

'Nor me,' he confessed. 'I keep thinking about things the way they used to be and wondering where I went wrong.'

'You didn't,' Thea said wearily. 'I did.'

Gavin regarded her contemplatively from behind his own desk. 'I don't suppose,' he said on a tentative note, 'it's any use suggesting we try it again?'

'I don't think so.' She found a smile. 'Thanks anyway.'

'It would be better than pining for someone you can't have,' he insisted. 'Dave's committed to Blaire.'

She eyed him sharply. 'He told you that?'

'As a matter of fact, it was Blaire herself. Seems they've had this understanding for years that one day they'd marry. She says it was Dave who suggested this trip to the States in the hope she'd be ready to settle down when she got back. Apparently she is. So you see it's no use. He belongs to Blaire. You belong to me—or you did. You could again if you'd let yourself.'

'Gavin?' Her voice was very low. 'Did you ever really want me? Physically, I mean.'

He stared at her, nonplussed. 'What kind of question is that?' he asked, sounding faintly embarrassed. 'Of course I did.'

'You never showed it—at least, not to any extent.'

'What was I supposed to do—try wheedling you into bed with me?' He shook his head, eyes bleak. 'I leave that to people like Dave. I imagine he's very good at it.' The pause was brief. 'Isn't he?'

Thea felt the telltale colour spring in her cheeks. She could hardly bring herself to meet the hazel eyes. 'How did you know?'

'The way you've been acting since I got back. The way you look sometimes when you think no one's watching you.' His tone was dry. 'If he weren't so much bigger than me I'd sort him out.'

She was looking at him as though she had never seen him properly before. 'And knowing it, you'd still be ready to take me back?'

'Yes.' He said it without hesitation. 'You were got at by an expert. I blame him, not you.'

'But you're still not willing to tackle him about it?' She was being unfair and she knew it, but the urge was too strong. 'Some champion!'

His gaze didn't drop. 'You took away my right to be one. Give it me back and who knows what might happen. After all, you know what they say. The bigger they are——'

'I'd never ask any man to fight because of me,' she said. 'You were right the first time anyway. He'd flatten you.'

'I'd risk it if I thought it would get me anywhere. I do love you, Thea. Perhaps not as forcefully as you'd like, but it's real enough for all that.'

'Oh, Gavin!' She hardly knew what to say. 'You deserve a better wife than I'd be.'

'I don't know about what I deserve,' he came back. 'I just know what I want. Highfields is like Sculla in miniature, with the added advantage of being within easy reach of civilisation.'

'You don't think we're civilised on Sculla?'

'Not in the same sense. The atmosphere here is insidious. It creeps into you—makes you reluctant to do anything new or different. Getting this job has given me a whole new outlook. It could give you one too. Why not take a few days when I leave at the end of my month and come and see for yourself? There'd be no obligation.'

By the end of another month she might well be wrapped up in another kind of dilemma, Thea reflected painfully. She doubted if he would react to that with quite the same tolerance.

'I'll think about it,' she said.

Any doubts she might have had regarding the seriousness of Dave's threat were resolved for her that evening when she saw her father. The senior members of the Rourke family were away on holiday, he said, leaving only Cousin Jenny at home. He hadn't thought she would want to make the visit under the circumstances. Thea agreed it would have been difficult, and told him not to worry as she had already had second thoughts about leaving the island. Whether he believed her or not she wasn't sure, but he seemed relieved by her attitude.

Her mother said nothing about the affair, simply watched her with sad eyes. She thought a lot of Gavin, and had looked forward to the day when he would be part of the family. Thea longed to confide in her, but knew she couldn't. The burden was hers and hers alone.

She was grooming Lady on the Saturday morning when Blaire turned up. The South African girl was riding the grey gelding, legs clad in jodhpurs and boots.

'Gavin loaned me some of his mother's gear,' she said, indicating the latter. 'Luckily we take the same size in footwear. He said you know some good places to swim?'

She knew some bad ones too, Thea reflected, thinking of another weekend not so long ago. 'The best one is on the west side of the island,' she said. 'But if you don't feel like riding several miles, there's a very sheltered little cove about ten minutes away. If you take the lane back there as far as the grey stone cottage, then cut up through the wood, you'll come out at the right spot. The path down to it is a bit steep, but it isn't dangerous providing you watch where you're going.'

'Supposing you come and show me?' the other girl suggested. 'I could use some company.'

Thea glanced up at her, slim and elegant as she leaned against the door of the shed that was Lady's stable, dark hair caught back from her striking features in a casual knot at her nape. 'Is Dave neglecting you?' she asked lightly. 'Shame on him!'

'He's tied up this morning. Later we're going across to the mainland to find some entertainment. I suggested making up a foursome with you and Gavin. He said to ask you.'

'Gavin and I aren't a pair any more,' Thea replied unemotionally, and saw the dark brows lift.

'So what? You're still friends, aren't you?'

'Well, yes, but——'

'No buts. It would do us all good to get off the island

for a while. I don't know how you stand being hemmed in here on a permanent basis. There's so little to do!'

If one more person said that to her, Thea thought, she would scream! 'We have very simple tastes,' she retorted.

'You must have.' Just for a moment there was a hint of acridity in Blaire's voice, quickly smoothed out. 'At least come for a swim.'

Thea went back to her grooming. 'I'm sorry,' she said, 'I'm tied up too. After this I have to muck out.'

'Then we'll talk right here.'

Thea kept her voice level with an effort, not pausing in her movements. 'Talk about what?'

'Not what—who.' The pause was fleeting. 'Dave isn't the same guy any more. I'd like to know what changed him.'

'I didn't know him before he came here,' said Thea, 'so I'd hardly know what you're talking about.'

'Oh, I think you do. I'd even go so far as to say you'd a great deal to do with it.' She came over and took the curry-comb out of Thea's hand, expression determined. 'If you and Dave are having an affair I've a right to know about it.'

'Then why not ask him?' Thea suggested.

'Because he wouldn't be likely to tell me.'

'And you think I will?'

'You already did.' The blue eyes were cool. 'He's only been here a month. How long has it been going on?'

Denials were useless; she had already given herself away. Thea shook her head. 'It isn't like that.'

'You're trying to say it only happened once?'

There was pride in the tilt of the fairer head. 'That's right. Once.'

'Then why all the——' Blaire stopped abruptly, expression taking on sudden dawning enlightenment. When she spoke again it was in a tone of resigned acceptance. 'So it finally caught up with him.'

Thea was silent, not understanding—unable to believe that anyone could react the way Blaire was reacting to something like this. Given a reversal of roles she was certain her own response would have been very different.

'Doesn't it bother you any more than that?' she got out.

'You mean that he made love to another girl?' Slim shoulders lifted. 'He never was any saint. The point is you're not just any other girl.' She paused briefly, eyes steady on Thea's face. 'It was the first time for you, wasn't it? The very first, I mean.'

This, Thea thought, had gone far enough. She reached out and took the curry-comb back from the unresisting hand, face stiffly composed. 'I've got work to do.'

Blaire didn't move. 'In other words, yes. That explains everything.'

'How?' Despite herself, Thea was drawn to ask the question. 'What does it explain?'

'Why he's acting the way he is. He said to me once that if he ever took a virgin he'd feel committed to marrying her. Don't ask me why—one of those quirks of human nature. If it had been anyone else but Dave I'd have laughed it off, but he doesn't say things he doesn't mean.' Her smile had a faint edge. 'I'm surprised he hasn't already done something about it. Or has he?'

'I've no intention of marrying him.' Thea's voice was low but surprisingly steady. 'No matter what happens. He's all yours.'

'No, he isn't. He never was *all* mine.' Blaire leaned an

arm along the door for support, mouth wry. 'Oh, yes, I could have married him if I'd played my cards right. He even suggested it himself. The trouble was I didn't want to settle down right then—as a wife, I mean. Dave has old-fashioned ideas about wifely fidelity—maybe because his mother didn't practise it very hard. That's why I went away—to think about it.' The smile came again. 'Apparently I left it too late.'

'It isn't too late.' Thea put comb and brush together and stacked them away on the shelf above the door. 'I already told you that.'

'You don't seem to understand. He doesn't go back on his word easily. If he hasn't asked you to marry him yet, he will.'

'I don't *want* him!' The vehemence startled the mare, causing her to jerk her head, almost pulling the headstall strap from Thea's fingers. She calmed the animal with soothing noises, stroking her nose until she stood quietly again. Only then did she finish unfastening the buckle to slide the band off, sending the mare out into the field beyond with a light slap on the rear, then following her.

Blaire had opened the door wide to allow the animal free passage. Now she swung it closed and latched it. 'You're protesting too much and too loudly,' she said. 'You must feel something for him. You'd like Natal.'

'I like it here.' Thea's tone was muted this time. 'And here I'm staying.' She pushed a distracted hand through her hair. 'I shouldn't be talking about it at all.'

'I don't see why not. You obviously need someone to talk to.' Blaire paused, resignation in her eyes. 'Look, I'm not doing myself any favours saying this, but you could do a lot worse than marry Dave. He'd give you everything a woman could want.'

'Including love?' Thea had said it before she could

stop herself, biting her lips because it gave away so much.

There was a certain sympathy in the other eyes. 'Ah, now that might be something else. You see, Dave genuinely believes love makes fools of people—blinds them to everything but what they want to see. It certainly did his father. He was the last to know what kind of woman he'd really married.'

Thea looked at her for a long moment. 'Was knowing that part of the reason you were so doubtful about marrying him?'

'Well, no. As a matter of fact, I feel pretty much the same way.' Her mouth curved ironically. 'There were other factors involved. We're compatible in some departments. Comparing him with other men I met these last few months, I finally realised I couldn't do any better. What I didn't bargain for was you.'

'I pose no problem, I can assure you. There's nothing would persuade me to marry him now.'

'Then you're a fool. You could have it all. Working from the inside you might even manage to change his attitudes. Anyway, he doesn't take no for an answer very easily—you must have realised that much.'

Thea picked up the broom leaning against the shed and opened the door again. 'He can't force me into anything. That's something *he* has to realise.'

'Have it your own way.' Blaire went back to where she had left the grey tethered and got into the saddle, lifting a hand in brief farewell. 'I'll make sure he gets the message,' was her parting shot.

She wouldn't dare tell Dave they had had this conversation, Thea tried to reassure herself; failing because Blaire Westwood was obviously capable of anything. How he might react she hated to think. She didn't feel too proud of herself for having admitted so much.

Knowing what she did know now about him was no help at all. If anything it made things worse. He and Blaire suited one another down to the ground. No way was she going to come between them. No matter what happened, she told herself fiercely, she wouldn't marry him!

It was chiefly for her mother's sake that she made herself attend the social that evening, putting on a determined cheerfulness which got her safely through the inevitable comment her split with Gavin elicited. By now news of his intended desertion had already filtered through the grapevine, splitting the islanders into two factions composed of those who understood his reasons and those who believed he owed it to Sculla to stay on regardless. Of the first, the general consensus of opinion was that Thea should go with him, while others applauded her decision to stay. She was relieved when suppertime brought a break in what was for some becoming a regular battle of words.

'People are worried about the kind of man we might get in Gavin's place,' confided the Vicar, cornering her as she stood drinking coffee at one of the windows during the interval. 'Has Mr Barrington gone into it yet?'

'He's going up to London to interview several candidates next week,' Thea told him. 'He'll choose the right man for the job, you can be sure of that.'

'It should really be his duty to do the job himself,' he said, shaking his head. 'After all, he's the trustee.'

'But he has a home of his own to think about,' she pointed out automatically. 'And Sculla isn't everyone's ideal.' She glanced at the bland face next to her. 'Do you ever feel restricted here, Mr Conniston?'

'Restricted?' He considered the question quite seriously, head on one side. 'Well, no, I can't say I do.

Perhaps a little when Mary and I first came here. Before
this we had a parish in Birmingham, you know. It was
quite a change.'

'Would you go back, if you had the opportunity?'

'To Birmingham?' He smiled a little. 'Obviously
you've never lived in a big industrial city. No, if it comes
to a choice I'll take Sculla any time. People here live
simple lives and commit simple sins—if any. No mug-
ging, no raping, no promiscuity.'

Thea's cheeks burned suddenly. Perhaps fortunately
he wasn't looking at her, his attention diverted by
someone over by the door. 'Mr Barrington! We were
just discussing your plans for Whirlow.'

Thea didn't turn round; she couldn't. She put the
coffee cup to her lips and made some pretence of drinking as Dave came over to where they stood.

'They're well in hand,' he said. 'A week sees the builders arrive.'

'I was thinking more about the future,' the clergyman
replied. 'You really can't see your way to making your
home with us permanently?'

'I'm afraid not.' The regret was in the words only.
'Someone told me only recently that home is where the
heart is.'

'And yours never left your own country.' Mr
Conniston sighed. 'Well, no one can blame you for that.
I just hope you manage to find a good man to take
your place. Ah, there's my wife beckoning. You'll excuse
me?'

In the small silence which followed his departure,
Thea couldn't think of a single thing to say. It was left
to Dave to make the first move.

'I want to talk to you,' he said. 'Not here. In private.'

She lifted her head then and looked at him, attempting
to read the expression in his eyes without success. 'I

thought you were taking Blaire to the mainland?'

'Blaire doesn't have priority,' he returned. 'Right now we're going somewhere to talk.'

'I don't think so thanks.' She was conscious of her mother's eyes on them from across the other side of the room, along with others. 'We're attracting enough attention already without creating more.'

'Taking you out of here by force would create one hell of a lot more.' He hadn't raised his voice one iota, but the tone said it all. 'Which is it?'

He would do it, she knew. In this mood he was capable of anything. 'Why now?' she asked desperately. 'You've had all day.'

'Blaire only told me she'd been to see you about an hour ago. I was going to leave it over till tomorrow, but it won't wait.' He moved impatiently. 'Do I have to go and ask your father's permission to talk to his daughter? I've got the car outside. We don't have to go anywhere but that.'

It was easier to give in than to argue further. Thea caught her father's eye as they moved to the door, and gave him a reassuring little smile, willing him not to come after them. She had to handle this herself.

The car was parked at the rear of the school. Seated in the front of it, she waited for Dave to get in beside her, schooling herself to calmness. They would talk, but that was all. If he touched her she would get out.

He sat for a moment or two just looking straight ahead into the darkness before he spoke. 'You and Blaire had quite a chat this morning, by all accounts.'

'She told me you'd asked her to marry you not all that long ago,' Thea acknowledged, feeling the pain of that statement even as she made it. 'I think you should do it. You seem to share the same outlook.'

'That was one of the reasons,' he said levelly. 'She

told you our land adjoined?'

'Yes.' A frown creased her forehead. 'You mean it was going to be a business arrangement?'

'Not altogether. We have enough in common to make it a workable proposition. Blaire inherited Tall Trees when she was nineteen after her parents were killed in a car accident, but she's never been all that interested in farming, so I've been more or less running the place alongside my own for the last six or seven years. She wouldn't let me buy her out. She wasn't sure she wanted marriage at the time I suggested it, so I told her to go away and think about it.' His head had come round now turned towards Thea. 'That's partly why I was such a long time coming over to see the place. I thought she might get back in time to come with me. I didn't even know where she was to get in touch because she was travelling. In the end I took a chance that she'd eventually call in on a mutual friend in L.A. and sent a letter there to wait for her. What I didn't expect was that she'd turn up here.'

'A pity she didn't make it a few days earlier,' Thea observed with a surprising lack of emotion. 'It might have saved all this.'

'It might have postponed it,' he corrected. 'When I asked you to take that walk last Friday night I planned to tell you about Blaire and ask you to wait until I got it sorted out. The rain put paid to that.'

Thea sat very still. 'Are you trying to say you wanted me to marry you even before you——'

'Before I lost my head,' he finished for her on a wry note as she trailed into silence. 'That's about it. I needed to know how you felt about it before Gavin got back.' His smile came slow. 'Don't look so disbelieving. It happens to be the truth. I'd known since we got back from Penzance that I couldn't let you go back to Gavin on any permanent basis. Remember the first time we met aboard the *Molly*? You'd no awareness of yourself at all. I wanted to waken you up—make you realise there was more to life than any little island could offer. I tried to tell myself it was purely for your sake, but I had to admit it in the end. You were so far under my skin I couldn't get you out.'

'It sounds a terribly painful complaint.' Her voice was shaky. 'Dave, is it true you don't believe in love?'

'I don't believe in all the mystique attached to it,' he answered candidly. 'Nine times out of ten it's a euphemism for want anyway. I want you, Thea. We can be married quietly in Penzance, then come back here for a few weeks until I get things sorted out. Once that's done we'll go back to Natal. There's so much I want to show you out there.'

'You're going too fast.' It was little more than a whisper. 'I can't——'

'You can.' He reached out and drew her to him, cradling her face between his hands as he kissed her long and lingeringly on the lips. 'And you're going to,' he added, moments later. 'Aren't you?'

'Yes.' She was beyond saying anything else, her whole body trembling to his touch. Dave didn't love her now the way any woman dreamed of being loved, but that wasn't to say he couldn't learn. Wasn't it Blaire herself who had advocated fighting from an inside position? 'Only not right away,' she added. 'How do you think Gavin is going to feel if we're working together in the same house? It's only been a bare week since we broke things off.' She hesitated, not liking the look on his face. 'Couldn't it wait till we're ready to leave Sculla altogether? It would be so much easier all round.'

'For who?' he asked dryly. 'Am I supposed to wait a couple of months to make love to you again? Last time was too quick, too spur-of-the-moment. I didn't get the chance to show you what it can be like. If it wasn't for Gavin and Blaire, I'd take you back to the house right now!'

'I'm not asking you to wait,' she said. 'I'm not even sure I could myself. All I'm asking is that we postpone getting married until we're ready to leave Sculla. Is that so much?'

'Not when you put it that way, I suppose.' He sounded resigned. 'All right, we postpone the wedding.'

Thea rested her cheek against the broad shoulder, savouring the possessive feeling it gave her. 'What about Blaire? When are you going to tell her?'

'She already knows. She's leaving tomorrow.'

'You were that sure I was going to say yes?'

'I was that sure I wasn't going to let you say no.' From the sound of him he was smiling again. 'Unlike Gavin, I don't believe in letting the grass grow under my feet. What time does this affair finish?'

'Half past tennish.' She lifted her head to look at him uncertainly. 'You're not thinking of telling Mom and Dad tonight?'

'No, I'm not thinking,' he returned, 'I'm intending. The sooner the better.' He looked at his watch, reading the luminous figures. 'Just ten. We could go to the house and wait for them. You have a key?'

'It isn't locked,' she said. 'Nobody ever bothers on Sculla.'

'I'd forgotten—no crime rate. You're going to have some adjusting to do back home.'

His home, she thought, not yet hers. It still seemed unreal. Yet two months was long enough to get used to the idea. She had to get used to the idea if she wanted Dave, because he wasn't going to stay here, not for her or anyone.

They were in the house by ten minutes past the hour. Thea led the way through to the sitting room, nervous now in a way she had not been before. If Dave tried making love to her here she wasn't sure how she would react. The thought that her parents might walk in any time would be more than enough to put her off.

'Would you like something to drink?' she asked him. 'I think Dad has some whisky in.' She was opening the corner cupboard as she spoke, hand reaching for the half full bottle in some relief. 'Yes, here we are.'

'Leave it there,' he said. 'And stop flapping—I'm not going to start anything here and now, much as I'd like to.' He patted the cushion at his side on the settee. 'Come and sit down. I can at least hold you.'

She went gladly, sliding into his arms with a sense of belonging. Things might not be perfect, but feeling like this was surely a good enough start? She would teach Dave about love while he taught her about making it— the abstract against the physical. That hers was going to be the more difficult task she refused to acknowledge. He wanted marriage. That had to mean something. The rest was up to her.

The Ralstons came in at twenty-five minutes to eleven, forewarned by the car parked outside. Dave took immediate charge of the occasion, his arm about Thea's shoulders as he faced his future in-laws.

'We're going to be married,' he said. 'I thought it fair to tell you now rather than later.'

John Ralston was the first to speak, his eyes on his daughter's face. 'Isn't it rather sudden?'

She flushed faintly, knowing he sensed all was not the way it should be. 'I'm sorry if it's given you a shock.'

Her mother looked stricken. 'Does this mean you'll be going away after all?'

'Not for a couple of months,' Dave reassured her. 'And it won't be for ever. It's only fourteen hours by air.' He met the older man's eyes without a flicker. 'I'll take good care of her. She'll want for nothing.'

'I hope not.' The smile was stiff. 'I suppose we have to accept it. Can I offer you a drink to celebrate?'

'Not right now, thanks. I've a feeling you'll want to talk things over between you. Thea, will you come to the gate?'

She went too willingly, dreading the moment of return. There were going to be some pertinent questions to be answered, and she didn't feel up to them. Not tonight. She knew what she was doing, regardless of what others might think.

'I'll tell Gavin myself,' Dave said at the car. 'You're going to have enough to face. Don't let your mother make you feel guilty. She's had you for twenty-three years.' He bent and kissed her, running his hands down her back to pull her to him. 'I wish I were taking you back with me right now. I'd like to spend the whole night making love to you.' His laugh came low. 'Slightly over-confident, but the sentiment's right. Think you're going to be able to cope?'

'With practice,' she said. She wanted to tell him she loved him, but the time wasn't right for it. Take it as it came, she told herself.

'Tomorrow I'll be taking Blaire over to the mainland,' he said, 'but I'll be back early afternoon. I've had the *Queen* patched up. How about spending an hour or two getting her ready for re-launching?'

Thea knew what he was really suggesting. The *Queen* was one place where they could be alone. The thought of lying in his arms in the close confines of the cabin made her ache in anticipation.

'I'll be there at three,' she said.

'And I'll be waiting.' He kissed her again before getting into the car, looking at her through the opened window, an odd little smile on his lips. 'No backing out now. You're committed.'

In more ways than he knew, she thought, and watched the car out of sight before turning with reluctance to go back indoors.

CHAPTER ELEVEN

HER father was on his own in the sitting room, a tot of whisky in his hand.

'Your mother went up,' he said. 'She's not feeling very well. It's been shock on shock for her these last few days—first Gavin, and now this.'

'I'm sorry,' Thea said wretchedly. 'I know how much she thinks of Gavin.'

'But Dave means more to you.' He eyed her with a troubled expression. 'I thought it was all one-sided?'

'So did I until tonight.' She couldn't bring herself to fully meet his gaze. 'He's been waiting to straighten things out with Blaire first. Apparently they had some kind of understanding.'

'Until he saw something he liked better.' He looked down at the glass in his hand, obviously finding words difficult. 'Any man who changes his mind once can do it again. What guarantee do you have that this marriage of yours is going to last?'

'None,' she admitted. 'Who does? Did Mom ask you for a guarantee?'

His smile was faint. 'I was a different proposition. Your mother was the first woman I ever wanted to marry, and I knew she'd be the last. Dave's the kind of man women seem to find exciting. Even if he's willing to leave them alone it doesn't necessarily follow they'll leave him alone. Can you cope with competition?'

'I love him,' she said. 'That's all that matters to me.'

'But does he love you? There's a lot of men don't know the difference between lust and love, and the first is no basis for marriage.'

'I'll have to show him the difference if that turns out to be the case,' she defended stoutly. 'I'm going to marry him, Dad.'

'I can't stop you. Just think very hard about what it's going to mean. You'll be in a strange country with a man you barely know. If it starts to go wrong you'll have no one to turn to.'

'It won't go wrong,' Thea insisted desperately. 'Please don't say any more.'

'I don't think there's anything else I can say.' He sounded resigned. 'When is it to be?'

'Not until just before we go,' she said. 'An island wedding would be out of the question, especially while Gavin is still here.'

'I'm glad you've given him some consideration.' He paused, studying her, pain in his eyes. 'If Dave hadn't come here you'd have been happy enough with Gavin. It was a bad day all round when Douglas died.'

There had been a time when Thea would have agreed with that statement. Now she could only feel grateful for the fate which had brought Dave to her before and not after she had married Gavin. She hoped the latter might one day meet someone who would give him what Dave had given her. Then he might understand.

'I obviously wasn't meant to stay on Sculla all my life,' she said gently, 'but it will be good to know it's still here to visit. I know I love Dave more than he loves me at the moment, but I can do something about that. What I can't do is live without him. Not now. Try to understand, Dad.'

'I do. And I think he's a very lucky man.' His regard was steady. 'Just try to be circumspect these next few weeks, will you, Thea? For your mother's sake. I don't think she could take any more shocks.'

'Of course.' Her face burned. He was nobody's fool. If it should become necessary she would keep her secret until well after they had left Sculla, she decided there and then. There were doctors on the mainland she could go to.

Later, in bed, she thought long and hard about the possibility of having Dave's child, and found the prospect far from undesirable. Perhaps subconsciously she even wanted it to happen, she reflected just before she drifted off to sleep. It would give her a hold over him of a very special kind.

She was at the boathouse for three o'clock on the Sunday afternoon, to find Dave not yet there. When he did turn up around four she was on her knees polishing brasswork with a vigour which cloaked her emotions.

'I waited to put Blaire on the train,' he said, coming aboard. 'She said to tell you she'll see you in a couple of months.'

'Will she still be living next door?' Thea asked without looking up from her task.

'Only for a short time. She's promised to sell me the land.'

There was a brief pause before he came across the deck to where she knelt, taking hold of her under the arms to draw her to her feet. In the white cotton tee-shirt, with his hair roughened by the wind, he looked so devastatingly male it was like a blow to the pit of her stomach.

'Any problems?' he asked.

Thea thought of her mother's face at breakfast, and wished she hadn't. 'Nothing I can't handle,' she said untruthfully. She searched the strong features, looking for the kind of reassurance she knew she wasn't going to find. 'Did you tell Gavin?'

'Last night. He took it pretty well considering—said

I'd better make you happy, or else.' He was smiling. 'Are you happy, Thea?'

'Yes.' She said it with emphasis, almost with defiance. 'Yes, yes, yes!'

His gaze kindled suddenly as if he had been waiting for the right cue. 'Let's go below,' he said.

The cabin was dim, its berths made up for daytime use. Dave undressed her slowly between kisses, hands so gentle she was scarcely aware of his actions until the last garment was gone and she lay quivering and defenceless in his arms.

'You're beautiful,' he said, leaning on an elbow to study her. 'Long, lean limbs, a waist I can almost span—breasts just made for the palm of my hand! No, don't look away from me. There's nothing shameful in my seeing you like this.' He kissed her again, waiting until she relaxed before touching her, fingers tracing the lightest of passages across her skin. 'I'm the first,' he murmured into her hair, 'and I'm going to be the last. No other man is going to know you this way. Do you hear me, Thea?'

'I hear you.' Her arms were about him, hands shyly exploring the smooth muscularity of his back beneath his shirt. 'I don't want any other man.'

'That's good.' He sat up and pulled the shirt over his head, tossing it to one side, then slid out of the rest of his clothing with a total lack of selfconsciousness, smiling a little at the run of warmth under her skin. 'Now we're equal,' he said softly, coming back to her. 'No encumbrances, no restrictions—and all the time in the world!'

Whatever reservation was left in her vanished for ever during the space of that late afternoon. The first time, as Dave had said, had been over too quickly, leaving little to remember but the feverish need. This was different: a slow, sensuous build towards a climax which left them both physically and emotionally drained. Yet even at the height she found herself unable to say the words she longed to say, because Dave didn't believe in love. It was the one marring factor in their whole relationship. She could only hope and trust that time would change his mind.

It was later, after they were dressed again, that he said with decisiveness, 'I'm taking you up to London with me on Wednesday. I've only two interviews each day, so it will leave us plenty of time to spend together. I'll book a suite for three nights, and travel back Saturday.'

'Dave, I can't.' She said it with regret, already imagining what it would be like to spend a whole night in his arms. 'There's no good reason why I should be needed on this trip. People would talk.'

'So what if they do?' He sounded unmoved. 'It will be some preparation for September when I take you away altogether.'

'And what about my mother? She has to live here in the meantime. It isn't so important for Dad, he's more worldly anyway—but Mom——' She stopped, registering the stony quality in his expression with sinking heart. 'It would kill her!'

'Unlikely,' he said. 'Gossip is a menace, but it isn't fatal. I've already made one concession for Gavin's sake. Don't expect me to wait out two months without some compensation.'

'You can hardly call what happened this afternoon lacking in compensation,' Thea pointed out on a slightly harder note, and saw the grey eyes narrow suddenly.

'No, I can't,' he agreed. 'And how often do you think we're going to be able to come here to the boat before people start talking about it?'

It was a moment before she answered, resentment stirring in her at his tone. 'That would surely depend on how often we did come, wouldn't it?'

'Oh, you're so right.' His jaw had tautened ominously. 'Are you trying to suggest rationing me?'

'Of course not.' She was doing her best to remain calm and in control of the situation. 'But you could be reasonable.'

'What would you call reasonable? Once a week? Or even once a month, maybe?' There was a cruel line to his mouth. 'Sorry, darling, but I'm not cut out for long periods of celibacy.'

'In other words, I make myself available when you want me, or else!' she fired back at him. 'Well, I'm sorry, but I'm not a convenience. If that's all you're interested in, find yourself some other little fool to seduce!'

The silence seemed to stretch to infinity in the moments following. Thea stared at him aghast, hardly able to credit that things could have gone so wrong in so short a time.

'I didn't mean that,' she got out, hating the still, hard look about his face. 'I really didn't!'

'Why not? You're perfectly right. I set out with the full intention of having you, one way or another.' He looked at her assessingly, no hint of tolerance about him. 'Do you want to call the whole thing off?'

'No!' The denial was a small cry of pain. 'Dave, I——'

'Then you've two choices,' he went on inexorably. 'Either you come with me on Wednesday, or we get married regardless of anybody's feelings. Which?'

'That's not a choice,' she said huskily. 'It's an ultimatum.'

'So it's an ultimatum. I've tried pleasing you, now

I'm going to please myself.' He got to his feet, tucking shirt into waistband with hard hands. 'You've got till tomorrow to decide.'

Don't go, she wanted to say. Not like this. But the words wouldn't come. This was another side of the man she loved; a side she didn't care for. 'There goes a man who likes his own way,' Janine Barrington had said of him. How right she had been!

It was a long evening, made even longer by her mother's lack of vitality. If even the thought of losing her only daughter could do this to her, what would the reality be like? Thea wondered in depressed concern. That was if she finally went. Considering the way Dave had acted this afternoon there was an element of doubt. To live with a man who tempered dominance with love was one thing, but without the latter emotion it could become too much.

She spent a sleepless night trying to work things out in her mind, rising at six no nearer to a solution. All she could hope was that Dave would have undergone a change of heart and be prepared to see matters in a more reasonable light. If he hadn't—— She could not bring herself to think beyond that point.

Gavin was already in the office when she got there. His greeting was diffident.

'I suppose congratulations are in order,' he said. 'You got what you wanted after all.'

Had she? Thea wondered. Or was it only what she had imagined she wanted? She would know when she saw Dave.

It was gone ten before he came in, looking lean and fit in white cotton jeans and close-fitting brown shirt. He made no attempt to come over to where she sat, leaning his weight against the edge of the other desk to eye her with an unreadable expression.

'Gavin, I'd like to talk to Thea alone,' he said. 'Do you mind?'

'Do I have any choice?' asked the younger man with uncharacteristic dryness.

Thea waited until he was out of the room before saying softly, 'Do *I* have any choice, Dave?'

'The same one you had yesterday,' he returned without a flicker of emotion. 'One of two.'

'One of three,' she corrected after a cold moment of decision. 'We can call it *all* off.'

His lips twisted. 'For someone as concerned about public opinion as you are, wouldn't that be rather shortsighted? Especially considering the odds have shortened some more.'

It was the first time she had even thought about that particular aspect—the first time she had thought about it at all since Saturday night, She gazed at him in dull acknowledgement; unable to find any way round what he was saying.

'As a man of experience, shouldn't you have considered that beforehand?' she got out. 'Or don't you care?'

'I can't say I'd mind all that much,' he admitted. 'It's time I was thinking about a son and heir.'

'If I refuse to marry you it won't make any difference.' There was a quiver in her voice. 'You can't have everything your own way, Dave.'

'No, that's true.' His tone was surprisingly mild. 'But I'll have one or the other. Are you coming to London with me?'

Her teeth closed painfully on her lower lip. 'No. Neither am I accepting the alternative. I'll take my chances on my own, thanks.'

'If that's what you want.' The grey eyes had gone steely. 'Book a room at the Connaught, if you can get it. Three nights. And make it a double—I might feel like consoling myself.'

He was gone before she could comment, closing the door forcefully after him. Thea resisted the urge to run after him only by bringing all her willpower to bear, biting her lip until she tasted blood. It was over. No matter what happened now, it was over! To marry a man like that would be tantamount to handing over control of her whole life. She would go away if it became necessary, somewhere neither Dave nor anyone else could find her.

She was working without visible sign of distress when Gavin returned. If he had any notion at all of what had taken place he kept his own counsel on the subject. There was no one she could turn to, she thought, no one she could ask for advice. She almost wished Blaire back again. At least the other might be able to tell her where she had gone wrong.

It was raining when she went home; a fine drizzle just enough to grease the roadways without washing them clear of accumulated dust. Her mother was in the kitchen where she was normally at this hour of the day. On impulse, Thea went over and put her arms about her waist from the rear, resting her cheek against the unresponsive back. There was nothing she could say to comfort her. Not yet. She might still have to go away in the end.

The rain stopped before supper was over, but it was too dull and overcast to tempt her into taking a ride. After settling Lady down for the night, she went back home and took a warm bath, lingering longer than she was accustomed to doing in an effort to soak away some of the depression that threatened to swamp her. Dave hadn't been near her again all day. He had even been missing at lunch. So far as he was concerned, she had made her choice, and he wasn't going to argue about it.

Thinking about it in retrospect, she began to see aspects she hadn't paused to really examine before. She was the one who had refused to contemplate an early marriage. And why? Because of other people's feelings. Having gained his agreement to a postponement, could she really expect him to sit back and wait for her permission to enjoy what he had already known twice? Self-assertive he might be, but ordinary pride had played as great a part in what had passed between them, both this morning and yesterday afternoon. If anything was to be salvaged at all, one of them had to back down. What she had to ask herself was did her feelings for him go deep enough to make her the one to do it.

The answer had to be yes in the end, because life without him was more than she could bear to contemplate. It couldn't be more than nine o'clock, she thought. Why not go and tell him now? Did it matter so much that he couldn't say the same words back? His love was of a different kind, that was all. He would show her instead.

She was dressing when she heard the phone start ringing downstairs. It was as if some premonition stilled her hands, holding her there in suspended animation as she listened to the muffled sound of her father's voice when he answered it.

The tread of his feet on the stairs a moment later was half anticipated, his knock on her bedroom door wholly so. She went to answer it, looking up into concerned eyes with a face as white as a sheet.

'Dave had an accident in the car,' John Ralston said. 'Apparently he skidded on the drive and hit one of the entrance pillars. That's all I know as yet. You'll want to come with me, of course.'

'Of course.' She was moving as she spoke, her

emotions numbed. He couldn't be dead, she told herself. Not Dave. She would know it by now if he were.

They reached Whirlow in minutes, to find a small crowd gathered around the slewed vehicle. There didn't appear to be very much damage, Thea saw with relief as she slid out of her seat. Just a badly smashed front wing.

They had taken Dave out and laid him on the grass on a blanket fetched from the house. He was still unconscious, the dark abrasion at his temple testifying to the cause. She watched her father examine the injury, saw him run his hands over trunk and limbs to test for breaks, then nod to the men standing waiting.

'Right, let's get him up to the house. We'll use the blanket as a makeshift stretcher. Each take a corner and lift when I say.'

It was only as Thea straightened that she saw Gavin standing there looking singularly helpless.

'I'm sorry,' he said, looking at her pale stricken face. 'I'd no idea what to do. He'll be all right. Your father will take care of him. He'll be all right, Thea!'

Providing there was no fracture, she thought. He must have hit the dashboard a tremendous crack to be out this long. She walked beside the little party on the way up to the house, searching the face on the blanket for any sign of revival, but finding none. He was as still as death, the powerful body shorn of its strength.

With the patient deposited on his own bed, Dr Ralston attempted to despatch Thea from the room along with the rest, but she shook her head.

'I'm staying,' she said flatly. 'Is there a fracture?'

'I'd say not,' he stated cautiously, probing the area, 'but it's difficult to be certain without X-rays. He's been unconscious more than half an hour, though, and that isn't good. There's bound to be concussion—I shan't be sure how severe until he comes round. Take off his shoes, will you. We can at least make him comfortable. I shan't attempt to get that sweater over his head tonight, though. He can sleep in it.'

Thea slid off the brown leather shoes and peeled off his socks, refusing to stand back while her father struggled to lift the inert body and take off the fawn slacks. They pulled the covers over him together, father and daughter working in unison. If only he would move a limb, or even groan a little, Thea thought looking down at him, not just lie there so utterly without life apart from the shallow rise and fall of his chest. Not a heavy, laboured breathing, thank goodness. At least that was a good sign. It was difficult to tell if his colour was returning under the tan of his skin, but it looked warmer—more relaxed. Sitting on the edge of the bed, she reached for one of his hands and pressed it to her cheek, willing him to open his eyes and look at her with recognition.

'You're already lovers, aren't you?' her father asked softly, watching her face.

'Yes.' She didn't turn her head. 'I love him so much it hurts. Do you know what that feels like?'

'Perhaps not to quite the same extent,' he admitted, 'but I can imagine.' He waited a moment before going on. 'You said the other night that you felt more for him than he did for you. Do you think you're going to be able to live with that knowledge?'

'I can live with anything,' she said, 'providing Dave is a part of it. I've been such a fool, Dad. I was putting everyone before what he wanted. We quarrelled today, and it was all my fault. If he still wants me when he wakes up, I'm going to tell him I'll marry him as soon as it can be arranged.' Her eyes met his frankly. 'I'm sorry if Mom and Gavin have to suffer a little gossip because of it, but Dave has to come first. I can't ask him to wait until we can safely leave Sculla in someone else's hands.'

'Your mother will survive,' he said. 'So will Gavin. I'm not going to pretend I don't feel some animosity towards a man who couldn't keep his hands off my daughter, but being one myself I do have some inkling of how difficult that can be at times. I——' He broke off, his attention turned back to his patient. 'I think he might be starting to come round. His eyelids moved a little then.'

The prediction was proven a couple of moments later when they moved again, this time opening slowly to their full width. The grey eyes were blank for a second or two until they came to rest on Thea's face.

'Hi,' he said faintly. 'I thought I heard your voice, only it seemed to be coming from a long way off. What happened?'

'You skidded in your car,' she said, 'and hit your head.' She was still holding his hand. Now she put it to her lips and kissed the back of it just below the wrist, feeling the fine hair tickle her nostrils. 'I love you, Dave. I'd have wanted to die myself if you'd been killed!'

'I'll leave you,' said her father, getting to his feet. 'Only not for long. I'll need to have another look at you later, Dave. You're concussed.'

'I feel it.' He hadn't taken his eyes off Thea, the expression in them hard to define with any accuracy. 'Thanks, John.'

Thea waited for the door to close, then bent forward to put her lips very gently to his, kissing him with all the pent-up agony of the last hour.

'I thought I'd lost you,' she whispered. 'I really thought I'd lost you!'

'Not a chance.' His smile was faint, but the strength was returning to his limbs, the fingers she held turning their grasp on her in no uncertain terms. 'You know, I could hear you and your father talking even before I could open my eyes. I'm starting to remember what you were saying too.'

'You don't have to remember,' she said. 'I'll repeat it.' Her tone was steady yet with an underlying uncertainty that wasn't lost on him. 'I told Dad I was a fool for not marrying you when you wanted me to—for letting other people come between us. I said I'd marry you any time you said, if you still wanted me.'

'There was more to it than that.' His eyes were narrowed, mind turning inwards. 'You said you knew you felt more for me than I did for you. What exactly did that mean?'

'What it appears to mean.' She smiled and lifted her shoulders a little in a wry expression of acceptance. 'You don't believe in love the way I do. To you it's all physical. Actually, I think you're afraid to let your emotions take over, because that would make you vulnerable—the way your father was.'

Something stirred in the eyes watching her so intently, some flicker of expression only he knew the full meaning of. 'Tell me about the way *you* feel,' he said. 'Tell me how it differs.'

'In depth,' she responded. 'In degree. If you never made love to me again I'd still love you the same way.'

'Liar!' The smile was stronger this time, mocking in intent. 'You need it as much as I do.'

'Only because you bring out that side of me.'

'The real Thea Ralston.' His voice taunted, but there was tenderness in it too. 'Cool, calm and collected on the surface, but wild as they come in bed!' His grasp on her hand tightened. 'Come here.'

'No,' she said determinedly. 'You're concussed, and you mustn't be excited.'

'I'm going to get excited,' he growled, 'if you don't do as you're told. Obedience is one of my prime requisites in a wife.'

'I know.' Still she made no move. 'That's one of the things we're going to have to sort out later when you're feeling better.'

'I never felt better.' Dave pulled her to him, his hand slipping behind her head to hold her as he kissed her. 'Just get in here with me and I'll prove it to you,' he murmured a moment later, sinking back into the pillows. 'Not quite my usual performance, perhaps, but I'd cope.'

'Magnificently,' she agreed. She had her cheek against his chest, listening to the strong beat of his heart. 'Better than most men at any time.'

A hand came up again to curve the back of her neck in a caress that made her own heart quicken its beat still further. 'What would you know of most men? I'm the only man you know—the only man you'd better ever know!'

'You're the only one I want,' she said, turning her lips to his jaw. 'Why can't you accept it? I *love* you, Dave. Whatever that lacks in meaning to you, it means everything to me.'

'Oh, God, Thea.' His voice was so low she could barely hear it. 'What did I ever do to deserve you!'

She was silent, not trusting herself to speak, waiting for him to say something else. Anything else.

'You know,' he added after a lengthy moment or two, 'I've spent my life believing all women were basically the same as my mother—and treating them that way too. My father loved her without ever knowing her as she really was until the very end. When she left I was twelve, just old enough to have some idea of what it was about. Dad filled me in on the rest.'

'He had no right,' Thea murmured without lifting her head. 'He should have kept his bitterness to himself. He's as much to blame as your mother was for the way you think.'

'The way I thought,' he corrected. 'Not any more. Not about you, at any rate.' His hand was inside her shirt, possession in its touch. 'You're what I need, Thea. Not just your body, every last part of you. I was on my way to tell you so when I hit the post. The very first time I saw you it was like having a flame lit inside me. I can't put it out. Is that love?'

'Close enough.' He was fanning the flame inside her right now, more than she could bear. She caught at his hand, stilling its movement, her mouth soft and full. 'Dave, this can't be doing you any good. Does your head hurt?'

'Like hell,' he said. 'And I don't give a damn. We're getting married the minute I get hold of a licence. Gavin will just have to grin and bear it. I want you here at Whirlow with me these next few weeks—day and night. Particularly the nights. I've hardly slept this last few.'

'Nor me,' she confessed. 'I'll come to London with you too, if you want.'

'No.' He moved his head on the pillow, wincing as he did so. 'Let's not give your mother too much to cope with at once. I'll come back on Friday, we can be married on Saturday. Sorry if you've always yearned for a white wedding, but I don't think you're really entitled. The honeymoon will have to wait too, I'm afraid. Once I've got things settled here we can go anywhere you like.'

'Providing you're there,' said Thea, 'I don't really care.' She disengaged herself gently but firmly. 'I'm going to call Dad back in. You need attention to that head.'

'Damn my head!' his brow furrowed, but his tone was still forceful. 'Just don't go away. I want you here, Thea.'

'I'll be here,' she promised. 'I'll always be here.'

As long as we both shall live, she thought, going to the door.

THE BEAUTY OF PENZANCE

A long finger of land jutting into the Atlantic from the southwest corner of England, the beautiful county of Cornwall has been discovered by thousands of vacationers. And one of the most popular spots in Cornwall is the historic coastal town of Penzance.

With a history that dates back to the pre-Christian times of the Celts, Penzance is steeped in ancient lore and tales of shipwrecks and smugglers. Dwellings more than two thousand years old still stand, attesting to the town's long history. As well as being the birthplace of Sir Humphrey Davy, the inventor of miners' safety lamps, Penzance is also known for its two museums and library, which contain many records of Cornish history.

Tucked into the sheltered southern shores of Cornwall's Penwith Peninsula, Penzance provides a sharp contrast to Cornwall's chilly and rugged northern coastline. Here in the warmer climate around Penzance, palm trees and other subtropical plants thrive, surely creating the most unusual setting in the British Isles.

One spectacle invariably included in British travel books may be seen from the shores of Penzance: St. Michael's Mount, a famous breathtaking castle perched on a rocky crag rising out of the sea. At one time the castle was a Benedictine monastery; but before that, according to local legend, the Mount was part of the lost kingdom of Lyonesse, where King Arthur's knights once rode.

FREE!
Romance Treasury

A beautifully bound, value-packed, three-in-one volume of romance!

Romance Treasury

An exciting opportunity to collect treasured works of romance! Almost 600 pages of exciting romance reading in each beautifully bound hardcover volume!

You may cancel your subscription whenever you wish! You don't have to buy any minimum number of volumes. Whenever you decide to stop your subscription just drop us a line and we'll cancel all further shipments.